MURDER IN GETTYSBURG

To Nancy,
Hope you enjoy.

Chucknepper

CHARLES H. KNEPPER, JR.

This book is dedicated to my wonderful wife, Leslie.

Special thanks to my Ninth Grade English Teacher, Ms. Kay Yaukey.

ISBN: 978-1-300-41785-9

Chapter 1

I slipped the cap onto the nipple and eased back the hammer. As it clicked into the fully cocked position, I carefully raised my head up and peered over the ridge. Steadying the heavy Enfield rifle, I raised it and took careful aim at the advancing rebel. Taking a deep breath, I let out half of it, held the rest, and slowly squeezed the trigger. The hammer fell smartly onto the percussion cap. The heavy rifle boomed and pushed hard into my already sore shoulder. Squinting through the cloud of arid white smoke that engulfed me, I saw the gray clad body fall. My god, I thought. I've actually shot him.

I didn't have time to dwell on my feat. I knew the confederates were still coming. Pickett's brigade, we'd been told. Almost mechanically I reached into my ammo pouch for a red paper cartridge and bit off the crimped end. I spit out the small piece of paper and poured the contents down the already hot barrel. I quickly peeked over the ridge again to check on the action rapidly unfolding right in front of me. There were bodies strewn all over the battlefield. The rebels were still advancing. Just as I reached into my cap box, a twelve pound Napoleon cannon on my right roared and hurdled backwards from its recoil. The good old Napoleons were bronze and smooth bore so they didn't pack the punch of the newer, rifled Parrots, but they were still impressive when they let loose.

With my rifle caped and cocked as before, I took aim at another one of the faded gray uniforms marching towards my position. I pulled the trigger. The front of the rifle jumped and the hard wooden stock slammed into my shoulder again. This time, however, my target didn't fall. I saw the rebel soldier aim his rifle directly at me. Flame and smoke exploded from the muzzle and a split second later I thought I heard the boom. That was the last thing I heard before I hit the ground.

Chapter 2

"Come on, dude. You going to sleep all day?"

I barely heard the voice. I slowly opened one eye. Looking up I saw the blurry outline of another individual. My entire head throbbed and the face above me kept spinning around like an old 45 rpm record on my turntable back home.

"Would you please stand still?" I said.

"I am standing still. What the hells' wrong with you?"

"Wow, man. I feel like I just spent all three days at Woodstock. My head is killing me………"

"Well, look, the battles over and we've got to get going; take a couple of aspirins and you'll be fine. Come on" replied the other man.

The cobwebs slowly cleared from my head. I finally managed to get the other eye open. I lifted my head slightly and slowly shook it from side to side trying to finish clearing it. I slowly looked around at the remnants of the battle. Men wearing both blue and gray were walking side by side towards the parking lot. Others were taking down tents or parking caissons and loading cannons onto trailers. A few were still lying on the grass where they had fallen.

My name is Gerry Campbell. Me and my best friend Bill South are avid history buffs. Unlike some folks, we decided to carry our interest in the War Between the States a heck of a lot farther than the average history student. We've been part of a local Union regiment doing Civil War reenactments at county fairs, community get-togethers, and actual battlefields up and down the east coast. The "battle" we had just waged commemorated the anniversary of the battle of Gettysburg. Nobody actually got hurt, but it was a great way to relive those exciting times and gain some insight into how people lived a hundred and fifty years ago.

"You should get an academy award for that performance, old buddy" said Bill. "You looked like you really got blown away there."

"I feel like I really did get blown away" I replied as I got shakily to my feet. I looked around the lush, green battlefield and rubbed the back of my head. "My bloody head is killing me."

"No wonder" Bill exclaimed, looking at my head. "Your head actually is bloody. You must have really cut yourself. Turn around and let me have a look."

I looked down at my hands. They were covered with blood. I turned so that Bill could get a better look.

"There's a little still oozing out, Gerr. You haven't lost all that much, but it'll still probably stop once you lose twelve pints or so" he said with a hearty laugh. "Hey, over here must be where you landed. There's blood on that rock". He bent down for a closer look. "Yep, I'd say that's what did you in. Looks like your hard head cracked the rock, too."

"Very funny" I replied sarcastically. Let's go get me patched up and hit the road."

Bill and I walked over towards the first aid tent in silence. We were both totally exhausted. The battlefield was strangely quiet now. Minutes before the noise had been deafening. Cannon crashing, muskets booming, soldiers screaming.

Spectators had had to cover their ears from the non-stop noise. Kids had squealed, partly from fright, partly from pure excitement.

"Look at that guy" said Bill, pointing to one of the reenactors still lying where he had fallen. "Looks like he decided to take a nap before going home."

As we got closer the prone body stretched out limply on the ground, a chill began to run up and down my spine. It was a strange sense that something was terribly wrong. I was really concerned about the unnatural way the man seemed to have fallen. I quickened my step as we got closer.

"What's wrong, Gerr? Holy cow! I..........."

For the first time that I can remember, Bill was at a loss for words. The man lying on the ground in front of us had a gaping hole where his stomach used to be. Blood covered the wound and dripped into a dark red pool on the left side of the body.

"Is he..........?"

"He sure looks like it" I said. I bent over the man and reached down and with the first two fingers of my right hand I felt the vein on the left side of his neck. I was sure it was futile, but I guess it's pretty much an automatic response when you see what looks like a dead body. I mean, I guess it's what people expect you to do.

"I'm not getting anything" I said. "I'm not a doctor but I'd say he's dead. I can't understand how this could happen."

"Are you sure he's dead? I mean, like, are you positive? Maybe you should check again. You might have missed something."

"Hey, I was in the military, remember? I've seen dead before. This guy is really dead, take my word for it. Now, let's go find a cop."

Chapter 3

"Anybody know who he is?" asked the Pennsylvania State Trooper bending over the body.

"Never saw him before. Listen, can we go now? We'd like to get home sometime today, ok?" asked Bill.

"Sorry, guys" replied the trooper as he stood up ramrod straight. "The detective is on his way and you can't leave until he says you can leave."

Just as he finished with that statement, I saw a late model, brown, four door sedan come into my peripheral vision. It came bouncing across the green carpeted field to where the body lay. It was easily recognizable as a police car by its plain, pie plate hubcaps, drab paintjob, significant lack of chrome, and multitude of radio antennas. It skidded to a halt and the driver's door flung open. A medium sized man wearing a Pittsburgh Steelers jacket jumped out.

"Well, corporal, what have we got here?" was the first thing out of his mouth.

I surveyed the newcomer with a bit of distain. He didn't look anything like a cop should look. He reminded me of an aging hippie instead of someone we could be trusted to "protect and serve". He had long brown hair tied into a ponytail. He also had a brown matching beard that showed signs that the graying of middle age was quickly approaching. Under the jacket he wore a Grateful Dead T shirt and had on faded blue jeans stuffed into knee high moccasins. I figured Bill wouldn't have a very high opinion of him either.

"There's been an unfortunate accident, sir" replied the state policeman as the newcomer leaned over to examine the body. "These are the two who actually found him."

"Good, have the CSI folks been called?"

"You bet, Dave. They're on their way."

The man turned towards Bill and me. He reached into his left inside jacket pocket and pulled out a leather case. Flipping it open he revealed a shiny gold badge in the shape of a shield. The words "Detective" and "Adams County CID" were engraved on it.

"I'm Detective Sergeant Morrison. Can you two tell me what happened here?"

"I didn't know Adams County had a Criminal Investigative Division" I said, totally ignoring the question.

"We're a relatively young organization. With all the new folks moving into the area from the city, we're seeing a fairly big rise in crime. So, the powers that be, in other words the commissioners, decided we needed a Criminal Investigative Division. Now, what can you tell me?"

"Well, we really don't know much, detective. We were fighting this battle and when it was over, we found the dead guy laying here. That's about it."

"Yeah, I can see that. Now how about starting at the beginning and tell me everything. Starting with your names, for example. You can call me Dave, by the way."

"Ok. My name is Gerry Campbell and this is my good friend Bill South. We're from South Mountain. Its west of here; out by Caledonia."

"Yeah, I know where it is. Go on."

"Well, we belong to this organization that puts on reenactments of battles from the War Between the States. All of the units that do this are resurrected regiments that actually fought in the war."

"Wait a minute. I thought Gettysburg was a Civil War battle. What's this War Between the States thing?"

"The north called it the Civil War; the south called it the War Between the States. The south was actually correct. A civil war is technically between two different factions inside a single country. This was a war between two different countries, the United States and the Confederate States. Now as I was saying, we happen to belong to a Union outfit in Waynesboro. It's sort of like a club that does these things as a public service. Anyway, we all got together Friday and drove over here. We set up an authentic campsite for the tourists to visit. Then we actually sleep here on the battlefield. We keep everything as authentic as we possibly can. It's called "living history", if you know what I mean."

"Yeah" said Bill. "We camped here and put on demonstrations all weekend. Then this afternoon everybody got together and reenacted the battle. Well, not the entire battle. We only had two hours to get it all done so we just did the Pickets Charge part. We still have to break camp and get home. So if you don't mind, we'll be getting along now."

Morrison ignored him and kept questioning us. "I take it being authentic doesn't include using real bullets, does it?"

"Of course we don't use real bullets" exclaimed Bill indigently. "What the hell do you think we are, crazy?"

"Well, somebody used the real thing" answered Morrison dryly. "Now all we have to do is figure out if it was done by accident or on purpose. Tell me, how do you guys go about shooting each other in these make believe battles?"

"Are you saying it might be murder? How do you figure?"

"Look, I'm not saying one way or the other. And besides, I'm the one who's supposed to be asking the questions. You guys do want to get home sometime tonight, right?"

"Yeah, ok" I said. I figured we might as well go along with this guy or he might keep us here all night. "We simply pour a measure of powder down the barrel. We don't even use the ramrod for fear of an accident. Then we just put a percussion cap on the nipple and pull the trigger. The gun goes bang and lots of smoke comes out. That's about all there is to it. See here, I'll show you."

I picked up my rifle and handed it to the detective.

"There you go, the standard Union Army issue firearm. Fifty eight caliber Enfield rifle. Heavy as hell. Here's what you do. Take this little paper cartridge. Tear or bite off the crimped end and pour the powder down the barrel. During the war there would also have been a bullet in that paper cartridge. That's right, good. Now, take this cap, watch out, don't drop it. Cock the hammer halfway back and put it on that little nipple. Ok, now pull the hammer all the way back. Aim at something and let her rip."

All of this completed, the detective pointed the rifle across the field and pulled the trigger. White smoke and flame erupted from the muzzle as the rifle boomed and echoed throughout the now still fields.

"Not bad", said Morrison. "So that's how it works. How many guys were out here shooting these antiques at each other this afternoon?"

"Well, let's see, there were about three thousand Yankees and oh, hell, I guess about the same number of Rebs."

"And how many spectators?"

"I'd say close twenty thousand, more or less" I replied.

"Oh, great, six thousand suspects and twenty thousand witnesses. Damn, I love this job."

Chapter 4

The voluptuous blond was making her way slowly over to my table. Her ample bosom strained against the low cut neckline of the red satin dress she wore. Hard, perky nipples pushed outward on each breast. Her tight, round buttock gently swayed from side to side as she seemed to simply glide between the chairs. I politely rose from my chair as she approached.

"Would you like a drink?" I asked.

"I'd just love an apple martini" she replied coyly.

As I looked desperately from side to side, trying to get the attention of a waitress, an annoying buzzing sound reached my ears. I tried ignoring it but it only got louder. The blonde bombshell slowly began to fade as the buzzing grew even louder still. All of a sudden my eyes snapped open and the noise, unbearable now, seemed to be right in my ear. I cautiously lifted my head and surveyed the room. Same old story, I thought to myself. The gorgeous girl gets just so close and I wake up. Rolling over, I slammed my right hand down on the button on top of the alarm clock and the annoying buzzing sound stopped.

I sat up on the edge of the bed and just as my feet touched the floor, I felt a throbbing pain in the back of my head. Rubbing it gingerly, I figured I'd better find something for the pain or I'd never get anything accomplished all day. I went to the bathroom and pulled open the medicine cabinet. I found the aspirin bottle straight away, but had to fumble around with the childproof cap for several moments. I was finally rewarded when two of the little white tablets fell out into my eagerly waiting hands. I left the cabinet door hanging wide open and stumbled towards the kitchen.

The pills quickly disappeared followed by an ice cold glass of tomato juice. I hung my head over the sink for a few minutes waiting for the pain to subside. Miracle drug, my ass, I muttered out loud. This could take a while.

Just then the phone burst into song. I grabbed it on the second ring, vainly trying to keep my already pounding head from exploding into another round of intense pain.

"Gerr, old buddy. Are you up?"

"No, Bill. I'm still chasing that foxy blonde. Of course I'm awake. You think this is a recording or something?"

"Awfully touchy this morning, aren't we? Still having the dream about the dynamite chick, huh? Hey, turn on your TV right now! Channel 25."

"Ah, come on, Bill. I haven't had any coffee yet. Gimme a break, Ok?"

"Do it, Gerr. This is really important."

I crossed the living room and dug around in my couch for the remote. Finding it, I flipped on the high def 60 inch JVC. As the picture faded in, I was shocked to see the face of the dead man from yesterday staring out at me. Only the man was wearing an Air Force uniform with a silver star on each shoulder and enough ribbons on his chest to choke a horse. The sound arrived just as the reported was finishing up.

"To recap our top story, retired Air Force Brigadier General Wilford Malcomb was killed yesterday in a freak accident during a reenactment of the Battle of Gettysburg. Watch for further details in our Eyewitness reports at 12 noon and 6 PM tonight."

I put the phone back to my ear.

"Did you see that? It's all over the news, even CNN and Fox" Bill cried excitedly. "A retired general. How about that?"

"Pretty wild stuff" I replied. "Listen, I have to run some errands. I'll talk to you later, Ok? Bye."

As I hung up the phone, I thought pensively to myself; yeah, it is pretty wild stuff.

Chapter 5

I stuck the key into the dashboard mounted ignition switch and twisted it clockwise. The powerful 427 cubic inch V8 snarled into life. Almost immediately it settled down to a low rumbling idle. I figured since it was a nice day, I'd put down the top. While it warmed up, I reached up for the windshield clips and unlatched the front of the convertible top. Grabbing the center handle, I lowered it into the recessed well behind the seat.

I had bought the Malibu Blue 1967 Corvette Sting Ray convertible many years ago when I was only an airman in the Air Force. I don't have to tell you how much a sacrifice it had been trying to afford such an expensive purchase on an airman's' paycheck. But somehow I toughed it out and now that I'm retired, the car's worth several times what I originally paid for it.

I grew up locally in Waynesboro. I guess I had a typical middle class, post World War II childhood. Dad worked for the government and mom was a stay at home housewife. I did fair in school, well enough to make the honor roll once in Junior High and once again in Senior High. Nothing to write home about.

I thought about getting into sports in High School, but I was way too small. I weighed something like 95 pounds soaking wet. Not the ideal weight for winning letters.

I've been a gear head as long as I can remember. Dad used to take me to all the local car shows. Of course, back then when you went to a car show, they consisted mostly of 1920's and 1930's vintage autos with a few from the 1940's thrown in. It was at these events that I developed a lifelong love affair for the true classics, especially the prewar Packard's and Duesenberg's. Later, in my twenties, I was lucky enough to actually own a Packard.

Like most boys growing up in the 1960's, I used to build model cars. When I hit my teens, I began tinkering with the real thing. I started with a few old American autos but, unlike the other guys my age, I never really got into muscle cars. Oh, I drove enough of them but I was drawn more towards sports cars.

I bought an old MG and rebuilt it. I started racing it and became fairly successful. I moved up to a 2 litre Datsun roadster and finally ended up racing a Jaguar XKE roadster.

I met Bill while we were both in the Boy Scouts. We started out in different troops. Both of us were helping out our respective Cub Scout dens as Den Chiefs when we met at a conference. I guess you could say we immediately hit it off and became lifelong friends. We pretty much spent our teen years hunting, fishing, and camping. After High School, Bill left the local area and became a professional fire fighter. I stayed around the area for a while, but after being laid off from my job, I joined the Air Force.

Initially, I only planned to stay for one enlistment. They sent me to Vietnam, thankfully at the time when the war was slowly starting to wind down. When I returned, they sent me to the sunny, white sand beaches of Florida's Space Coast. I spent most of my spare time there surfing and deep sea fishing with my friends in the dormitory. It was here that I bought the Corvette.

Well, soon it became time for another assignment. I said to myself, Gerr, you really should go somewhere they speak the same language, since learning Vietnamese hadn't gone especially well. I put in for assignments in both England and Australia. I lucked out and got three wonderful years in outback Australia.

I had put on a little weight since High School so I thought I'd have a go at some of the local sports. I tried Australian Rules Football but decided I was much too sane for that sport. Figured Cricket and Softball were more my speed. I also did a little opal mining in my spare time.

After leaving Australia, I enjoyed a tour in Louisiana. Then I spend three wonderful years hunting and fishing in Alaska. Then I went south to sunny, historic San Antonio before finally ending up right down the road from Waynesboro at the Air National Guard base in Martinsburg, West Virginia.

During my time in uniform, I did find time to get in enough college for a degree in journalism. After I retired, I figured I might as well put that education to good use and started a new career as a writer. I always read voraciously and I figured if I could read, I could write. I started out small, doing the occasional article for the local newspaper and eventually I earned a weekly column. About a year later I broke into magazines. I started out with a few pieces for a moderately well circulated crime magazine. Finally I was rewarded with my dream job; a call came from the editor of my favorite automobile magazine offering me a position on their staff. I plan on keeping that job as long as they'll have me.

I wheeled the Corvette into the parking lot at Wal Mart. Just as I closed the door, my cell phone rang.

"Hey, Bill. What's up?"

"I just got a call; our new friend Detective Morrison wants to see us downtown right now."

"Where, downtown? Gettysburg?"

"No" replied Bill. "He's right down at the Chambersburg cop shop. He just wants more info."

"Ok, look I'm here at Wal Mart. I've got to pick up some photo paper to make some prints for an article I'm doing. I'll meet you there in about half an hour, no, hang on, give me forty five minutes. See you then."

Chapter 6

I idled the 'Vette around the corner and parked in the lot behind the police station. It was one of the newer buildings in downtown Chambersburg, having been built in the 1960's. A lot of the other buildings were built just after Confederate General Jubal Early burned the town in 1864. Bill was waiting for me in the small entrance foyer. We walked down the long hallway and found the front desk. As we got closer, the sergeant on desk duty waved to us.

"You two looking for Dave Morrison?" he asked.

"Yeah, know where we can find him?" replied Bill.

"Interrogation room right across the hall. He told me to make sure you went right in."

We pushed open the door and entered a room not much bigger than a fair sized shower stall. Detective Morrison sat at one end of a small wooden table with a chair on each side. He motioned for us to set down.

"Glad you boys could make it. My friends over here were kind enough to lend me the use of one of their rooms so you wouldn't have to drive the whole way to Gettysburg" he began.

"How could we refuse such a generous invitation from such a sweet guy?" answered Bill sarcastically.

"You don't like me very much, do you Mr. South?"

"I don't dislike you. You just don't look or act like a cop to me. It just doesn't seem right, if you know what I mean."

"Ok, look. I get it. I grew up in the '60s and I just feel comfortable dressing like this. Besides, I'm a detective. I'm not exactly supposed to look like a regular beat cop. And, I really don't care if you like it or not. Now, let's get down to business, shall we? Yesterday you guys told me the basics of your little war games. So tell me, how would a person go about getting a list of all the people who took part in yesterday's event?"

"Let's see" I said. "The victim, I suppose that's proper term to use here, was wearing blue. That means his killer was probably on the confederate side since it appears he was shot from the front. We can get a list of all the different units that participated and then you'll just have to get in touch with them for a roster of guys who were signed up for the battle on Sunday."

"Ok, that seems simple enough. And you're correct; he was shot from the front. We had the coroner burning the midnight oil to get the autopsy done. And of course, it was one of those nasty 58 caliber mini-ball type bullets you gave me that did him in. Problem is, we'll never be able to match it to any particular gun; it was too fragmented for that."

"Doesn't surprise me" said Bill. "Those damn things were awfully soft and traveled so slow that they just mushroomed into a big wad of lead or exploded into a million little pieces if they hit a bone. They sure mangled a lot of good men back then."

"Listen, I don't think I need to tell you two that this investigation is top priority. The public takes a very dim view of their war hero's getting whacked. My department is going to be under the microscope on this one and I'd like to solve it before the state boys or the feds step in and muddy the waters and bungle everything up. If you two can give me any help, I'd sure appreciate it. Oh, and while I think of it, did either of you guys have a wife or friend who might have been video taping your little battle for posterity? Maybe if we can come up with some tape of this thing, we might be able to find a clue somewhere."

"Well, I don't have a wife and Bill's too cheap to buy a video camera. But I'll tell you what we'll do. Wednesday is our unit's regular monthly meeting. We'll ask around. Somebody's bound to have a tape we can borrow, Ok?"

"That would be great. Thanks. In the meantime I'll see if I can find out if the general had any enemies, that is, besides the Viet Cong and anybody else that we've been at war with in the past thirty years."

The town of Waynesboro rests just north of the Mason Dixon line in the picturesque Cumberland Valley. The 139th Pennsylvania Volunteers hold their monthly meetings at the American Legion hall. It's an old, white painted brick building on the main street that runs east and west through town. Situated right next to the Police Station, the banquet room has been the site of many high school reunions, wedding receptions, and occasionally, even a wake or two. One Wednesday every month it catered to a group of make believe veterans of a war that took place eighty or ninety years before any of them were even born.

Instead of the usual business agenda and training classes usually conducted at the meetings, the talk invariably turned to the Gettysburg tragedy. When the call for new business came, I stood up and addressed the chairman, who is actually a well known Waynesboro attorney.

"Could I address the unit, Captain?" I asked. "I have a rather important matter to discuss with the troops."

"Certainly, sergeant. The floor is yours" replied the captain.

I walked to the front of the room and turned to face the unit. "Gentlemen, you may or may not know that Bill and I, sorry, Private South and myself were the ones who found the generals body. We've been asked to assist the detective investigating the case in any way we can. What we really need most right now, is your help. We're trying to locate any video tape or movie footage of the battle on Sunday. Did any of your wives or friends film the battle? This is really important, guys, and we promise you'll get your tapes back unharmed. We'll make copies and return your originals. Can any of you help us out on this?"

Several scattered hands went up around the room.

"I've got a tape you all can use" said a man old enough to be everyone in the room's grandfather.

"My wife got some good footage" answered another member.

A guy in the back shouted out that all of his film was at their disposal as long as it helped catch the low life that killed the general and cast a shadow of doubt across his beloved hobby. The public might begin to think these reenactments were too dangerous, he surmised.

Before the night was over, our members had pledged four complete tapes and several that contained just portions of the battle. I got everyone's address, telling them I would be around sometime in the next two days to pick up their tapes. We were due to meet with Detective Morrison on Friday.

Chapter 7

The second hand reached the twelve. I turned the key in the front door and pulled it out, and twisted the knob back and forth a couple of times to make sure the door was locked. Ten minutes till four. Any other Friday night I'd be picking up one of my lady friends, going to dinner, and then maybe to the club. So, what am I doing tonight? Spending it with Bill and the hippie cop. Oh, what the hell. Maybe, just maybe we'll catch this guy.

I could feel the moist dampness in the air hit me squarely in the face. I glanced up at the sky to see it was becoming increasingly dark and ominous. Black clouds were rolling in from the west with alarming speed. I knew we were in for a rather nasty thunderstorm. Probably already raining cats and dogs down in the valley.

I opened the Corvettes drivers' door and threw the bag with the tapes behind the seat. Settling into the driver's seat, I brought the big 427 to life. With the shifter in first gear, I eased out the clutch and the light blue convertible moved slowly forward. Turning right out of the driveway, I motored to the end of the road and made another right. About a quarter mile later, I turned onto Spruce Road and pulled into Bills' driveway.

"Looks like we're in for a pretty big blow, eh?" Bill said as he eased into the leather passenger seat. He always rode with me whenever possible. He had a perfectly good, reliable pickup truck but it was nowhere as much fun as my Sting Ray.

"Yeah, and it looks like it's already putting her down off the mountain."

I drove down the mountain and stopped at the intersection of Route 30. We turned right and started towards Gettysburg. I pulled the shifter back into fourth gear and the big V8 settled down into a smooth purr.

"Boy, I just love the sound of this baby" said Bill as the 'Vette cruised effortlessly down the Lincoln Highway.

"Don't forget the Corvette Meet at Carlisle is coming up soon. We are going, aren't we?"

"Of course. You know I never miss that show."

We kept driving east and reached the Gettysburg city limits about twenty minutes later. At the town square, all traffic goes in a circle around a large fountain. After waiting my turn, I entered the circle and followed it a quarter of the way around. I took the Baltimore Street exit and drove one block to the court house. Morrison's office was in the sheriff's complex in the basement. There's a parking lot reserved for the sheriff and his visitors with a dedicated entrance. I found a spot to park and pulled in. Don't worry about locking the car, I told Bill, if you can't trust your car in the police lot, where can you trust it? We entered the complex and found Detective Morrison waiting for us.

"How you doing, fellows?" asked the detective. "Ready for a long night?"

"As ready as we'll ever be" I answered.

The detective led us down a long hallway and stopped at a foreboding looking door at the end. He nodded to us. Pushing it inward, we were surprised to see a pleasant, but dimly lit room laid out like a combination military command post and New York recording studio. Along the left wall was a bank of computers, their screens emitting an eerie green glow. Straight ahead lay a mixture of teletype machines, fax machines, and telephones with dozens of twinkling red and white lights. Directly over these machines were several clocks mounted on the wall. Each one was adjusted for a different time zone. On the right wall was the video equipment. There was an assortment of machines representing all the various formats, complete with monitors and all of the assorted switches and cables. In the middle of the room was a huge three sided control module. I assumed this was a master panel from which any of all of the equipment in the room could be controlled.

"Well, guys. What do you think of our humble abode? We've got just about every setup imaginable here. Eight millimeter, standard VHS, three quarter inch pro format, DVD. There's even an old Beta machine over there somewhere. Plus all the equipment for cutting and editing that we could possibly use."

"I'm impressed" I said. "You could manage World War III from this place. Or produce a Hollywood blockbuster. Well, here's the tapes. Let's get this show on the road."

I opened the leather bag and pulled out the four complete video tapes. I handed the top one to Morrison. The detective pushed various buttons, made some adjustments, and finally inserted the tape into the VHS machine. Pushing the "Play" button, he settled back into his chair.

"Might as well relax, guys, this could take awhile. Now, remember, you two are the experts. If you see anything out of the ordinary, let me know immediately. I have no idea what I'm looking for, so I'm relying on you two."

We each pulled up chair to rest our feet on and began to watch the battle of the previous weekend unfold before us. Each tape was almost two hours long and presented a different angle of the conflict. We pointed out mutual friends and acquaintenances as the tapes wore on. We both were able to pick ourselves out from among the thousands of participants, commenting several times on my award winning dying act. All three of us watched intently for any videos of the general. He appeared briefly on all of the tapes but never long enough to see anything conclusive. Finally on the third tape, the camera operator seemed to have locked onto the generals unit and followed it throughout the attack. We saw the general advancing, sword waving high over his head. All at once, he appeared to stumble and then double over. He fell limply to the ground, landing in the position that Bill and I found him in. Using the high tech editing equipment, Morrison ran the tape forward, backward, slow motion, and even froze several frames.

"Well," said the detective. "We can see how he was killed and we know roughly when. What we don't know is who fired the fatal shot. Of course, we also don't know why he was killed. Maybe the rest of the tape will enlighten us. Might was well have a go at it."

He put the tape into motion again. We watched the rest without noticing anything unusual. Starting over, we ran through the tapes again. And again.

"Damn, I'm getting pretty hungry" said Bill. "What time is it, anyway?"

I glanced at the wall and located the clock marked "Eastern Time Zone".

"My god, its four thirty in the morning. We've been at this all night" I exclaimed.

"Unfortunately, there's not much open this time of morning" said Morrison. "There is a donut shop right down the street, if you're interested, though."

"How convenient, a donut shop a few hundred yards from a police station. What will they think of next? Let's go for it" replied Bill.

Morrison shut down the video equipment and closed the door behind us. The rain was over now. It had left the town glistening wet. We walked down the street to the donut shop. It reminded me of an oasis of light in the middle of a sea of darkness. The bright lights and smiling waitresses were in stark contrast to the rest of downtown Gettysburg which remained dark and foreboding in the early predawn gloom. I picked a booth near the front of the shop. Bill and I flopped down on one side and Morrison sat across from us. Bill distributed the menus while the detective motioned for the waitress. I ordered coffee and a cheese Danish. The other two placed their orders and we kicked back to await our food.

"You know," said Morrison, "I've got an appointment to talk with Mrs. Malcomb on Monday. She and the general live outside of

Pittsburgh. Well, at least she still lives there. You two want to be there for the interview?"

"Do we have to go there or is she coming here?" Bill asked.

"One doesn't ask the grieving widow to come to you; you go to her. I'm driving over about 8 am. Besides, I may be able to dig up a clue or two by nosing around the generals' house. You just never know. You interested in going?"

"I can't make it. Gerry can probably make it, though. He doesn't actually have a real job."

"Very funny. But, yeah, I can probably ride along. I've already submitted next week's article, so I do have some free time."

"Sounds good. I'll meet you at the station around 8."

Chapter 8

At ten minutes till eight I whipped the Corvette into the sheriffs' department parking lot. As I was unbuckling my seat belt, I could see Detective Morrison walking across the lot to meet me with a steaming cup of coffee in each hand.

"Glad you could make it" he said, offering me one of the cups.

"You want to take my car? We can put the top down and relax."

"Not that I wouldn't love to, but I don't think we should. If you don't mind, we'll take mine. It'll look a lot more appropriate if we drive up in a cop car."

"Sure, no problem. I just thought I'd offer" I replied.

We left Gettysburg traveling west on Route 30.

"So, Dave, where exactly does the widow live? You said it was outside of Pittsburgh?"

"Yeah, it's some fancy development in Monroeville. Know where that is?"

"You bet. Been there many times. I've got friends that live close there."

"Well before you ask, no, we can't drop in and visit them. It's a two and a half hour drive each way so we really don't have the time."

"I didn't ask. Hey, do you have the address?"

"Sure. Here it is." He handed me a scrap of paper with writing on it. "I think there's a map in the glove box. Check it out, will you?"

I pushed the lock button and the door popped open. I rummaged through the pads of paper, pencils, napkins from various fast food outlets, match books, and assorted items that always seem to take up residence inside the average glove box. Finally, near the bottom I found a dog eared map marked 'Pittsburgh and Surrounding Area'.

"I found one. It looks like it was printed during the Nixon administration; it still has Three Rivers Stadium listed on it. I suppose it'll have to do, though. Why don't you join the 21st century and buy a GPS unit?"

"I don't need a G-P-S; I have an M-A-P. They're a lot cheaper. Now, see if you can find Norway Lane. It's supposed to be in some development call 'Maple Grove Estates'."

I searched the map. Flipping it over I found the insert that highlighted Monroeville.

"I've got Maple Grove Estates" I said. "It must be a pretty old development to be listed on this map. I don't see a Norway Lane listed but I can get us to the general vicinity. We are on Route 143, aren't we?"

"Yeah, heading north."

"Ok, take a right onto Duke Street. It should be the next right. Then look for Jeff Davis Drive. It'll be on the left."

Duke Street came up much quicker than either of us expected. Morrison had to cut off a small red sports car in order to make the exit ramp. The driver held up one finger in response to the detective's sudden, unexpected move. I'll bet he had a few choice words for us, I thought. We drove on for close to a mile and a half when suddenly I saw the sign for Jefferson Davis Drive. I pointed it out to Morrison and he flipped on the left hand turn signal.

We entered one of the most beautiful neighborhoods I'd seen in a long time. Stately maple trees lined the streets. Huge southern style mansions sat in majestic splendor like guardians of a bygone era. Here and there a gardener could be seen trimming this or clipping that.

"So this is how the other half lives. Kind of makes you wonder, doesn't it?" asked Morrison.

"Yeah, now I'm really interested in seeing the generals' place" I replied.

Morrison continued driving slowly down the tree lined street. Between two of the larger trees on the right, we saw what appeared to be the entrance of a very large villa. A very tasteful sign proclaimed 'Maple Grove Estates'.

"This must be the place" I said. "Turn in here; we'll have a look around."

Morrison turned right and drove a quarter mile down the street. As we rounded a slight bend, a security guard stepped out of a small but rather elegant guardhouse into the street. The guard extended his left arm straight out with the palm of his hand pointing towards us while his right hand moved to cover the butt of the 38 caliber revolver he had holstered to his shiny black faux leather belt.

Morrison eased the car up to the guardhouse. The overweight guard ambled over to the car with a look of disdain on his face.

"Can I help you, sir?" the guard asked crisply.

"Why, yes. I believe you can" replied Morrison.

Reaching into his pants pocket, he produced his gold badge. "We're here to see Mrs. Wilford Malcomb on official police business. I'd appreciate it if you could direct us to her home."

"I doubt if she'll see you at this time. She'll be in mourning for quite some time, I'm afraid. Why don't you try back in a few months?"

"Look, bud. I didn't drive all the way over here to argue with some Boy Scout rent a cop with a freakin' cap gun. I talked with Mrs. Morrison on Friday and set up the appointment to see her today.

Now I suggest you call her and verify it before I put tire tracks all over your pretty uniform."

The security guard turned away and mumbled something under his breath. Returning to the guard shack, he picked up the telephone mounted conveniently on the wall just inside the door. Morrison and I decided to get out of the car to stretch our legs after the long drive. We could see the guard frantically talking to someone on the other end. Occasionally he would glance our way and gesture.

"What the hells' with all the hand gestures, I wonder. It's not like she can actually see him or anything" I said.

"Probably Italian. They talk like that all the time."

"Oh, that's real politically correct, Dave."

"Sorry, it just slipped out. What I want to know, is why he's getting so bent out of shape. It's none of his damn business who she sees and who she doesn't. It kind of looks like he's trying to talk her out of seeing us. Could be more here than meets the eye, my friend."

"Boy, that cop mentality of yours. Are you suspicious of everybody?"

"Can't help it. That's the way cops minds are wired."

We kept our eye on the guard while surveying the area. Beyond the guard house there were long, well manicured lawns and hedges with what appeared to be small groves of trees towards the back of each one. That must be where the houses are, I thought.

Just then my peripheral vision caught something move in the guard house. I quickly brought both eyes to the site of the movement. I saw the guard slam down the phone and reach for the doorknob.

"Here he comes, Dave" I said.

"Bout time he gets his fat ass out here" was Morrison's cold reply. "I don't have a lot of patience with these rent a cops."

The fat guard swaggered over to where we stood.

"Madam says to send you on up" he snarled. "Just bear in mind I'll be keepin an eye on you two, so don't be a givin' her any trouble, you catch my drift."

"Look, you fat little smart ass. I really don't give a damn if you like it or not. Just stay the hell out of my way, if you catch *MY* drift" Morrison snapped back while slamming his index finger into the fat guard's chest.

With that, he jumped back behind the wheel and slammed the door. I jumped in on the passenger side just as Morrison floored the accelerator and rocketed the car forward.

"Hey, be cool, man. He's only a rent a cop, remember?"

"Oh, I know it, but he just pisses me off so much. There's something I really don't like about him. It's not just his pain in the ass attitude, although that sure is enough to do it. It's something else; I just can't put my finger on it. But...........I don't know, it's just something. Maybe it'll come to me later on."

The detective slowed the car and relaxed. He kept driving down the long entrance road.

"You know, he never did tell us which house is the generals. How are we supposed to find it?" I asked.

"I guess we keep driving till we run out of road. There's got to be a sign or a clue or something somewhere."

We drove on for almost a mile. The road wound around gently to the right. Every so often a driveway intersected the main road. Finally they came to a large cul-de-sac. Directly in front was a stone wall at least twelve feet high that appeared to surround a large estate. A foreboding black wrought iron gate protected the entrance to the driveway which disappeared into a forest of tall green oak trees.

"Well, we've run out of road. Now what do we do?" I said.

"Good question. Hey, wait a minute. Look there. No, over this way." Morrison pointed towards the trees. "Back through those trees, see it?"

"Looks like an American flag to me" I replied.

"Right. And wouldn't a retired general proudly fly the flag every single day?"

"Yeah, you've got a point there. I should have thought of that. This could be the place. Let's go check it out."

We got out of the car and walked to the iron gate. Morrison nodded towards the small TV camera mounted inconspicuously on top of the wall almost obscured by an ivy vine that wound over the wall and into the gate. Underneath it, recessed into the stones, was an all weather speaker. Morrison walked over to the speaker. Before he could open his mouth, a female voice came crackling out of it.

"Mr. Morrison, I presume" asked the voice in broken English. "My guard has told me of your arrival. Please bring your friend and come up to the house. I'll open the gate."

"Fine, we'll be right there" replied Morrison. He turned and, gesturing to me, walked quickly back to the car.

After we were both inside, Morrison rolled up his window and motioned for me to do the same. Only then did he speak.

"It appears we're going to have to watch our tongue around here; this whole estate could be bugged, judging from the security just at the front gate. Let me do the talking and you listen very carefully, ok? You know more about the military than I do, so you might pick up something. Well, here we go."

Chapter 9

The heavy iron gate started to swing open on surprisingly well oiled hinges. Morrison put the car in gear and idled through the opening. Glancing in the mirror, he watched it close immediately after we had driven through. The narrow driveway led into the small forest we'd had seen from the street. Actually it was a misnomer to label it a forest. It was, more accurately, a large stand of trees planted around the house. And what a house it was. As we came out of the trees, the brilliant sunlight reflecting off the Malcomb mansion was blinding. I figured the house to be at least two hundred years old. It looked like the perfect stereotypical southern mansion of pre-Civil War days. I just had absolutely no idea why it was located outside of Pittsburgh.

"Looks like we went through a time warp, doesn't it? Or is this the sound stage for "Gone With the Wind?" asked the detective.

"I don't know, but I'll bet the president would trade the White House for this pad if he had the chance" I replied. "What the heck is 'Tara' doing this far north?"

Morrison circled the drive and pulled up directly in front of the huge front entrance. We got out of the car and climbed the wide marble stairs to the majestic, hand carved double doors. I reached out and pushed the button that sounded a rather unobtrusive, yet delightfully melodic doorbell. A tall black man impeccably dressed in a tuxedo, complete with white gloves, opened the door within seconds.

"Do come in, gentlemen" said the man with a decidedly British accent. "The mistress will see you at this time. She awaits in the drawing room. Please follow me."

We followed as the butler led us through a foyer large enough to play a high school basketball game. The butler stopped at another pair of double doors and knocked lightly. Upon hearing acknowledgement from within, the butler threw open the right hand door and stepped aside, bowing and sweeping his right hand downward with a flourish.

"Madam, the two gentlemen to see you" he announced.

"Ah, come in, gentlemen" said the same female voice with the broken English. "Randolph, you may go."

With that, the nattily dressed black man did a perfect about face and exited the room.

Damn, I thought. That move was military perfect if I ever saw one. I wonder if that fellow was ever in the service.

"Good morning, Ms. Malcomb. I'm Detective Sergeant Morrison and this is Gerry Campbell. He's acting as a professional consultant on this case. I trust you have no objections to him sitting in on our conversation?" said the detective as we entered the room.

We were greeted by a petite oriental lady, barely five feet tall. Her impeccably styled hair was jet black which only served to accent her extremely pale complexion. She bowed and motioned for us to sit on the couch opposite her chair, which we did.

"Ms. Malcomb, I know this is going to be extremely difficult for you, but I must ask some questions. Some of them may be rather painful to answer, but I assure you they are necessary to catch your husbands' killer. Now, did he have any enemies that you are aware of?"

"No, detective, of course not. I've tried over and over to think of someone who would want to harm my husband. But I can think of no one."

"Did your husband get into any business deals that you know of before or after retiring from the Air Force?"

"Oh, I would not know of these things. I am just a wife and a wife should run the house and leave the business to the man. Besides, when he retired, he just played a lot of golf and worked on his dumb old cars. He always said he didn't want anything to do with business. He was a warrior, not a businessman."

"I see. By the way, where did you meet the general?"

"We met in Vietnam. He was a captain then, flying F-4s, at least I think that's what they were called. My family was once closely related to the royal family; that's where most of the money for this estate came from, in case you might be a little suspicious. I met him at a club in downtown Saigon and we just seemed to hit it off, as you Americans say."

"Had he been doing the Civil War reenactments for long?"

"No, that was just his latest hobby. He felt that kept him in touch with his military past. He had only just started but because of his fame, they let him be the commander."

"I see" said Morrison. "Always the warrior, so to speak, even in retirement. Do you suppose we could look over the generals' papers? We might find a clue of some sort. I have to tell you, madam, we really don't have a lot to go on at the moment and I'd like to get started before the trail gets too cold."

"Of course, gentlemen. I quite understand. In fact, I'll escort you around the estate if you'd like and then you may have complete access to the generals den and all of his papers."

"That would be fine, Ms. Malcomb" replied the detective.

She got up from her chair and started across the room. We arose from the couch and followed her. She led us over to a large set of French doors and opened them onto a patio. The marble patio overlooked a crystal clear kidney shaped swimming pool. Two buildings were located farther back from the pool. A driveway led to the one on the left. We were taken, however, to the building on the right first.

"This," she said, waving her hand with a flourish, "was the stable in the horse and buggy days. We've never had any horses in here; the general wasn't very big on them. He said they belonged in the cavalry and he belonged in an airplane. We just use this building mostly for storage nowadays."

She led us around the side of the former stable to the rear. There was a path of grass cut much closer to the ground than all the rest. It had two white balls roughly the size of a softball resting on each side. Looks like a tee box at the golf course, I thought.

As if she were reading my mind, the generals' widow spoke. "The general was very fond of golf. In fact, it had become an obsession. He built four holes in the back yard; this is the tee off area for one of them. The flag is down there and the course circles around and finishes up over there behind the garage."

We followed her pointing finger and saw a red flag waving in the breeze some four hundred yards ahead of us.

She started walking towards the garage; Dave and I followed her.

"This is where the general kept his dumb old cars. I had an old one in Vietnam. Now I am in this country, I want a nice shiny new one, but no, he must have old ones. I do not understand."

She opened the side door and reaching around the corner, snapped on the light switch. Fluorescent light flooded the room. I blinked from the sudden flash of brilliance and then stared in disbelief. There were six classic automobiles lined up across the garage. On the end closest to me there was an early 1950s MG TD. Next to it was a 1957 Chevrolet convertible. Third place in line was reserved for any early 1970s Plymouth Barracuda convertible. Following that was a 1965 Shelby GT350. Next sat a 1964 Pontiac GTO convertible. On the far end was a heavily modified Corvette Sting Ray.

"My god" I exclaimed. "Ms. Malcomb, these aren't just some old cars. These are valuable collectors' items. They're worth a considerable amount of money. The MG and the '57 Chevy are everybody's favorites, the GTO is the original muscle car, and if I'm not mistaken, that 'Cuda over there has a factory hemi under the hood. Chrysler only made eleven or twelve of those. The Shelby is a classic in its own right. Now, I'm not so sure about the Corvette; it looks pretty heavily modified. I'd have to look a lot closer at that one. No, ma'am, these aren't just dumb old cars. These are works of art; rolling pieces of metal sculpture."

"Then, you actually *like* these old things?" she asked incredulously.

"Oh, absolutely" I replied. "May I look then over more closely? I'd love to check them out. This is what I do; I'm an automotive writer by trade."

"Of course, go ahead. Look them over all you wish" she said as she swept her hand across the room. "Take your time. I'll take the detective to the generals den so he can get started. Come back to the house when you've finished and

Randolph will show you to the den so you may rejoin your friend."

With that, she spun around and walked briskly back towards the house with Morrison in tow. I began to look around. I started with the MG. I'd always liked the TD models. My seventh grade math teacher had one. I ran my left hand slowly down the front fender, fondly remembering the first time I'd driven one. I took a friends for a test drive around Waynesboro one day when I was twenty one, considering whether to buy it or not. It was the first right hand drive car I'd ever had the opportunity to drive. Ultimately, I didn't buy it but I always remembered that day.

I walked over to the '57 Chevy. It was a glossy black Bel Air model with a white convertible top. The script 'Fuel Injection' was emblazoned on each front fender. Wow, I thought. This is a real rare piece. I decided I had to have a look. I stuck my hand under the front edge of the hood and searched for the release latch. I found it and pulled. The hood popped up slightly and I lifted it the rest of the way. Sure enough, there was the rectangular Rochester fuel injection unit sitting on the intake manifold. What a beautiful thing, I thought. I lowered the hood and then carefully but firmly pushed it the rest of the way down to latch it.

I moved over to the Shelby but not being a Ford man, I just gave it a cursory once over. I'd always been a General Motors man. I did want to look over the Barracuda, however. If it was a real hemi car, it was worth some serious money.

I gingerly lifted the hood and gasped. There it was. The 426 street hemi. The tire burning legend of all time. Coupled to the close ratio four speed gearbox with pistol grip shifter, this monster ruled the streets from coast to coast in the early 1970's. This 'Cuda was an extremely rare example of those bygone days. From my research and watching various auctions, I knew this car was worth a fortune.

I stepped over to the GTO. Ah, the big daddy of them all. The car that got the whole muscle car genre started. Again, I raised the hood and again I was greeted by a spotless engine compartment housing all genuine factory equipment. The 389 cubic inch V8, correctly painted Pontiac blue, sat there topped off with three, two barrel carburetors. I glanced inside to find this example also equipped with a four speed gearbox.

Finally I turned to the Corvette. I recognized it immediately as a 1963 model by the split rear window, the only year to have that particular configuration. It was also a former race car. It was blue with a white circle and the number 14 painted in black on each door and on the cars top. There was a bulge in the hood, probably to provide clearance for some exotic engine hardware, I figured. There were exhaust headers the size of sewer pipes sticking out of each side. As I wandered around to the back of the car, I noticed that it had a trunk lid. That's strange, I thought to myself. Sting Rays don't have trunk lids; I ought to know. I wonder why someone went to all the trouble to put one on a race car? You know, there's something strangely familiar about this car; I just can't put my finger on it. Oh well, I'm sure it'll come to me sometime. Better get on up to the house.

I walked to the back door of the mansion. Tapping lightly on the French door, I turned the handle and pushed it inward. I think I'd taken two steps when the butler, Randolph, appeared out of nowhere.

"You wish to join your friend, sir?" he asked.

"Yeah, if you don't mind" I replied.

The butler turned and stiffly walked out into the huge main room we had first entered. He started up the wide marble staircase towards the second floor and I followed, awestruck by the opulence surrounding me. Crystal chandeliers hung over the staircase. Rich teakwood handrails climbed the stairs on opposite sides and curved gently around the balcony at the top. The carpet on the second floor must have been two inches thick and was a deep maroon in color. I felt myself sink into it with every step I took. We turned right and went to the end of the hallway. Randolph reached the doorknob, gave it a turn, and pushed it open.

The heavy wooden door swung inward to reveal a den larger than my living room. The two opposing walls were lined with shelves packed full of books. There was a large hand carved desk centered on the back wall. This wall was filled with photographs, plaques, trophies, and other mementos from the generals' illustrious thirty year military career. Morrison sat in the overstuffed chair behind the desk poring over papers.

"Well, you done playing with cars and ready for some real work?" he asked, looking up from the papers that covered the desk top.

"Yeah, I'm ready. But let me tell you something, I don't know anything about the general personally, but he sure had some kind of class in the automobile world. That guy has some extremely valuable wheels out there."

"I don't know about valuable, but I found one of the bills of sale in this stack of papers. Here have a look."

I reached over the desk and took the paper from Morrison's outstretched hand. It was a receipt from a company called 'Classic Investments' with an address listing in Chambersburg, Pennsylvania. This particular receipt was for the Chevy convertible.

"Hey, this company is headquartered back home in Chambersburg. And did you see what he paid for that '57 Chev? It's rare, but not that rare."

"I saw it. About two hundred and fifty grand, wasn't it? It's a hell of a lot more than I'd pay. I'll tell you that."

"It's a lot more than anybody else would pay, too. Of course, a lot of people have no idea of the value of old cars. It's hard to tell what his rationale was. Oh, well. Back to work."

Both men returned to sorting through the mountain of papers. All the military paperwork went onto one stack, all the financial paperwork onto another. Paid bills went onto still another one.

"Hey, look at this" said Morrison. "Here's a prospectus from that investment company that he bought his antique cars from. Why don't you check it out while I go through these bills?"

"Sure, let me have a look at it. Maybe it'll enlighten us to that outrageous price tag."

I took the leather bound booklet from the detective, settled back into my chair, and began to read. After making my way through the document, I turned back to page one and reread the entire prospectus.

"Now I get it. These guys suckered him in, to put it bluntly. Either they're totally stupid, which I doubt, or they're some of the best con men on the planet, which looks more like the case. They've painted such an optimistic picture that anybody reading this would beat a path to their door, begging them to take their money. This thing says antique and collector cars will probably double in value within three years and quadruple in five."

"You mean they won't?"

"Of course not. Sure, they'll appreciate some. It's just like baseball cards. But they won't go up that fast. The figures those guys are quoting are just too far out there. Hey, don't get me wrong, it's an impressive document. But it's totally bogus. Remember, I'm a total gear head. I'm really into old cars. I write for car magazines. Bill and I go to the antique car shows at Carlisle and Hershey every year. We follow Barrett Jackson. We keep up on prices. I'm telling you, Dave, whoever wrote this was either smoking some of those left handed cigarettes or deliberately padded the figures big time. Heck, they've made it sound so good I'm ready to buy a car from them!"

"In that case, maybe we should stop by and see these folks on our way home. What do you think?"

"Sounds like a plan to me. You about finished there?"

"Yep. I've got everything sorted and packed in separate boxes. Let's just take it all and read it later."

With the boxes of papers safely stored in the trunk, both of us bid farewell to our hostess. She assured us that the gate would be open when we reached the end of the driveway. True to her word, as we approached, the huge iron gate began to swing inward. As the car drove through, it reversed itself and closed solidly behind us.

"There has got to be some outrageous security system hidden around that place. That old girl knew exactly where we were at any one moment, anywhere on the estate" said Morrison as we continued down the entrance road towards the guard shack.

"Yeah, pretty spooky wasn't it?" I replied. "Hey, look, there's your new buddy."

The fat security guard stepped from the building briefly as our car neared. Once he recognized the detective behind the wheel, he turned, expressionless, and reentered the building, slamming the door behind him.

"He's a real sweetheart, isn't he? I know he's one of my favorite people."

"Damn, Dave. Will you cut the guy some slack already? He's just a poor dumb jerk trying to earn his eight bucks an hour. Let's go talk to our big money friends at Classic Investments. Give me that map and I'll get us back on the Turnpike."

Chapter 10

The detective pulled into Chambersburg and turned into a Shell gas station. Retrieving the prospectus, he quickly looked up the address for Classic Investments. It was listed as Suite 810, Inverness Towers.

"Ok, Gerr. This is your town. Where's Inverness Towers?"

"Boy, I don't know, Dave. Remember, I live fifteen miles east of here. I don't actually spend a whole lot of time in town. Must be a fairly new building. I'm not familiar with that one. Why don't we ask that kid?"

"Hey, buddy. How do I get to Inverness Towers from here?" the detective yelled to the college kid pumping gas.

"That's easy, dude. Just keep going down this street till you come to Northeast Avenue. Inverness Towers will be the big building on the corner. Turn right and you'll go underneath to the parking lot."

"Thanks, kid. I owe you one."

Morrison rolled the window up, pulled the gear selector down into 'Drive' and, looking over his shoulder, merged into traffic.

"We've almost got it made, Gerr. A block or two straight ahead and we're there."

Within minutes we were driving under the building. We found a place to park and walked to the elevator.

"Well, I assume that Suite 810 will be on the eighth floor, right?" I said.

"That's normally the way they do it. Punch it up and we'll find out."

I reached out and pushed the button labeled '8'. It illuminated, the doors closed, and with a whirring of machinery, the car began to rise. The numbers clicked off at a rapid pace until they reached eight. The elevator car slowed, settled a bit, and finally came to a stop.

When the doors finally opened, both of us stepped out. A sign directly opposite the doors showed Suites 801-820 were off to the right and Suites 821-840 were to the left.

"Looks like we go right" I said.

We starting walking down the hall, watching the numbers on the doors rise the farther we walked. When we came to 810, Morrison knocked twice and waited. Hearing no reply, he grasped the door handle and twisted. To our surprise, it wasn't locked. The detective pushed the door open. The inside was in total blackness. Morrison fumbled to find the light switch. He flipped it on and the room was instantly bathed in brilliant fluorescent light. It was empty!

Almost empty, that is. There were a couple of chairs in one corner, a small table, one lamp, and several waste baskets.

"Real cozy office these big investors have here, isn't it?" said Morrison.

"This can't be the right place. You're sure you have the right number?"

"Y'all lookin fer ta rent this here room?" said a tired sounding voice from the doorway behind them.

Both men wheeled around, Morrison with gun in hand, to see a man in tattered clothes standing there. His unkempt gray hair made him look much older than he probably was. The faint smell of alcohol slowly permeated the room.

"Who the hell are you?" demanded the detective.

"Whoa, y'all don't need that there shootin' iron" stammered the old man. "I'm jus the janitor for this here buildin'. If you're a wantin' ta rent this here room, I'll have ta clean it up a tad fer ya first."

Ignoring his reply, Morrison asked "Wasn't there an investment firm in this office recently? I got this address from a friend who told me that Classic Investments really helped him score some big money, if you know what I mean."

"Well, that outfit was here. But they done cleared out lock, stock, and barrel 'bout a week ago. Didn't give nobody no notice or nothin'. Just picked up everythin' and done left. Damn near burnt the place down, too."

"What do you mean, almost burnt the place down?"

"Well, sir, shortly after they done left, the fire alarm went off. I comes up here and them two trash cans was just a blazin'. Like they had set them a fire on purpose or somethin'. I put em out, but ain't had time to clean it up. If ya want..........."

Morrison put his hand on the old mans' shoulder in mid sentence and steered him back towards the open doorway.

"Listen, we'd like to look the office over a bit more before we decide to rent. I know you're probably quite busy, so I don't want to keep you any longer than necessary. Why don't you go on about your business and we'll check back with you when we've made up our minds, ok?"

"That'd be right kind of ya, mister. I am powerful busy. Y'all just come down to the furnace room when ya done."

With that, he left the room and shuffled down the hall towards the elevator. I looked at the detective and smiled.

"That sure was a slick brush off."

"I just figured we didn't need an audience when we went through this place with a fine tooth comb. Let's check those trash cans first. There might be something left. You take that one and I'll take the other."

Each of us began examining a waste basket. The paint on the outside was blistered, the inside black with soot. There were, however, plenty of papers that hadn't been totally consumed by the flames. Apparently the sprinkler system and the old man had done their jobs much quicker than Classic Investments had figured.

"I've got some good readable stuff here. How about you?" I asked.

"Yeah, me too. Let's gather everything up real carefully. There might be some prints too, although I doubt it."

The detective reached into his jacket pocket and produced a couple of large plastic zip lock bags. He inserted the papers from his trash can into one of them and handed the other to me so I could do the same with mine. He then sealed both bags and returned them back to his pocket.

"Let's check out the rest of this place and split. I really don't want to try and talk my way out of this place again. The old guy might be a lush but there's an outside chance he could get suspicious. Let's figure on five minutes at the most.

We searched the rest of the office as thoroughly as possible in the limited time we had left. Nothing else of any substance turned up.

After checking the hallway, we turned off the lights and closed the door. The car was reached without incident. Morrison pulled out of the underground parking area and started for home.

"Well, do you think they were legit? I mean, most businesses notify the management when they decide to change addresses. And they don't try to burn their records, either" I said as the detective drove on.

"It sure looks odd to me. They left in quite a hurry. Right after the generals murder, too, if that old guys' memory can be trusted. We'll know more when we get back and examine these papers and the ones we found in the generals den" replied Morrison, patting the plastic bags resting safely in his jacket pocket.

Chapter 11

I didn't hear from the detective the rest of the week. That suited me just fine because Bill and I had plans for the upcoming weekend. And those plans didn't include playing amateur detective.

Every year the town of Carlisle, Pennsylvania hosts a dozen antique and classic automobile flea markets attended by hundreds of thousands of old car enthusiasts from around the world. With over eight thousand spaces for dealers, a person could generally always find whatever part they were looking for. We've made the trek religiously at least three times a year since the events inception over a quarter century ago. I was always looking for Corvette parts and Bill usually just checked the current prices and admired the restored classics. He loved the old cars but he just couldn't afford one at the moment. Never the less, he wanted to be ready just in case he hit that big lottery win.

I left the house early Friday morning. I picked up Bill and pointed the Corvette north. We had an hour cruise in the early pre-dawn darkness before we reached the small town of Carlisle.

"Did you and the hippie detective find anything interesting about the general's death when you went out west on Monday?" Bill asked.

"One thing we found out is, his widow won't be hurting for money. You ought to see the place she's living in. The guy had his own golf course in the back yard. And you should see his cars. He had an MG TD, a Shelby GT 350, a hemi 'Cuda, a Goat, a '57 Chevy fuelie ragtop, and some old 'Vette race car. I mean, he had some fine stuff. Oh, and get this; we found the bill of sale on the '57 Chev. Would you believe he paid a quarter of a mil for that thing?"

"Oh, come on. I'm calling BS on that. Nobody is going to pay that kind of bread for a '57. Even if it is a fuelie and a ragtop."

"No, I'm serious" I replied. "The general paid two hundred fifty thousand for that car. Well, we decided to go see the investment company that sold all these cars to him. And guess what? They had skipped out big time. Cleaned out their office and split. They tried to burn their company papers in some trash cans but the sprinkler system and an old lush the building keeps around as a janitor put out the fire before they were total ashes. Morrison's analyzing them now."

I pushed in the heavy duty clutch and slipped the shifter up into third gear. We had just gotten caught up in the seemingly endless stream of traffic heading to the Carlisle Fairgrounds. Cars of all types and eras were all slowly crawling towards the same objective. Just past the fairgrounds entrance, I suddenly turned right into a private driveway. The owner of the property, a smiling, slightly graying middle aged lady greeted us.

"Back again, I see. One thing I can always count on is you two showing up a couple times a year" she said.

"You bet. How much is parking this year?" I asked.

"Because I like you two guys so much, ten bucks. I wouldn't do that for just anybody, you know."

"We know; anybody else could park here for eight" I laughed.

"Ah, you guys know you couldn't park any closer to the gate for less."

"Just kidding, Mrs. Rozer. We know a good thing when we see it. Listen, we'd love to hang around and chat some more, but we'd better get going. Got to get there before all the bargains are gone!"

With a wave, I drove the Corvette around the house and into the back yard that served as a makeshift parking lot several times a year. We both knew Mrs. Rozer and all the other home owners in the area were making a small fortune parking cars at ten dollars a pop, but since it was only a fifty foot walk to the fairgrounds gate, everyone considered it a bargain. Being able to keep bringing heavy or bulky parts back to the car instead of lugging them around through eighty acres of flea market more than justified the expense.

I always considered locking a convertible a bit ridiculous, so we just made sure the glove box was locked and walked to the gate. After shelling out the seven dollar entrance fee, the back of both our hands were stamped with a bright yellow bingo marker. This way we could exit and reenter the event as many times as we wanted all day.

Long ago we had developed a systematic approach to attacking the flea market. We divided the fairgrounds into three distinct sections. We always visited the field closest the gate first. Next, we would walk the hill on the left, or the North field as it was called. The bottom field was always saved for last. I always figured, no matter what, if you looked for a particular part all day long, it was a sure bet that you'd find it in the bottom field.

Noon time found us halfway through the rows of vendors on the hill. After taking a brief break for lunch of the best barbecued beef sandwiches on the planet, we started out again. Every so often either Bill or I would stop at a booth to examine a part or leaf through some literature.

About two o'clock we found ourselves standing in front of a booth selling a mixture of new books and vintage automotive sale brochures. Bill was looking at some old brochures and I was checking out some books on a rotating stand out front.

"My god, there it is! That's the car!"

"What's the car? What the hell are you yelling about?" said Bill.

"That modified Corvette race car in General Macomb's' garage! Look at the cover of this book! That's it! It's not just some hacked up old race car; it's a Grand Sport!"

Bill looked over at the book I was holding. It was titled 'Those Fabulous Grand Sports' and had a full color picture of an early '60s Corvette Sting Ray leading a pack of Cobras into a turn on the cover.

"Yeah, right. Sure it is. Look, I've read about those things. They only made six of them and they're all accounted for. There's no way the general could have one. It's just not possible."

"I don't know how he got it, but he's got it. I know that's what I saw in his garage. Here, hold it while I pay the guy. I'm going to get to the bottom of this, once and for all."

Chapter 12

"I'm telling you, Dave, we've got to check out that 'Vette in the generals garage again. I've got to look it over close. Something's very wrong there."

"You can't be sure it's one of those Grand Sport things, whatever they are. Besides, you told me they only made six of them."

"Dave, I read this book from cover to cover" I exclaimed, waving the book I'd bought at the Carlisle show in from of Morrison's nose. "Man, I'm telling you that's what it is. It has to be. Look at these pictures."

Morrison glanced across the desk at the book.

"Gerr, look, I know what you're saying. But how can it be possible? You just told me they only made six of them and the book said each one is accounted for, either in a museum or a private collection. How could a multi-million dollar car that's so incredibly rare possibly show up in some retired general's garage, when there aren't even any of them missing? Did Chevrolet build an extra one and forget to tell anyone? Did somebody build a copy?" He paused, took a breath, and then started again. "Gerry, let me ask you a dumb question. I know it's possible to counterfeit money; is it possible to counterfeit cars?"

"That's not a dumb question. Sure, it's possible. Hell, for some cars it's downright easy. For certain models, all you have to do is tack on different trim or equipment. That's enough to change a standard, plain jane model into a much rarer, more desirable one in most cases. It happens every so often. You really have to check a car over good before you buy it. But you don't actually think someone faked one of the rarest cars in the world, do you? He'd have to know he would eventually be found out. I mean, that isn't nearly as simple as turning a standard Pontiac GTO into a Judge model simply by adding a few different decals. You're talking big dollars for that kind of job."

"I know, but it could be done, right? Let me lay a scenario on you. Suppose someone started selling genuine collector cars to the general at slightly inflated prices. And then let's suppose that when this someone realized that the general didn't have a clue as to their real value, this someone kept inflating the prices more and more. Now suppose this someone goes one step farther and counterfeits some collector cars and sells them to the general at even more ridiculous prices. Now this someone really has the general on the hook. Let's suppose this someone figures they can go for one really big score and then get out before the general gets wise. Make any sense to you?"

"Boy, you really do have a devious mind. I guess that comes with the job, huh? Yeah, it's not a bad theory. Not bad at all. In fact, it makes a lot of sense. Especially if this someone you referred to happens to be Classic Investments. And, obviously, it sure would explain why they skipped out so fast, too" I replied.

"Of course they'd have to have had a pretty solid setup, too. They'd need a garage or body shop and some pretty skilled workers for the actual work; they just sold the finished product."

"You know, maybe we'd better go back over to the general's estate and double check his cars. If your theory is correct, several of them are probably fake."

"You're right. We'd better. I'll call Mrs. Malcomb and ask if she'd mind if we come have a look. I know I'll never get a search warrant on my flimsy theory, so we'll just have to hope she voluntarily lets us come back. I'll try for this Wednesday. Will that work for you?"

"No problem. Meet you at the cop shop about eight, ok?"

"Ok, I'll call and make arrangements with the widow Malcomb, if she'll agree. If you don't hear from me, consider it a go. I'll see you then."

Chapter 13

Wednesday morning saw Detective Morrison and me make the same trip to Monroeville that we had made the previous Monday. This time, however, I came armed with a stack of books listing all the American cars made since World War II, including special models, special trim packages, and unusual options. They also identified each car by original vehicle identification number and engine number.

The general's widow met us as before and escorted us to the garage. She then excused herself, insisting we take all the time we need for a thorough examination of the general's collection.

"Well, Dave, you introduced me as your consultant the last time we were here; now is when I try to live up to the advance billing. Let's start with the MG and work our way down the line."

With that, I pulled out a pocket flashlight and went to work. I checked under the hood first. Then I proceeded to examine the car from bumper to bumper. Lastly, I pulled a round magnet from my pocket and stuck it to several spots on the cars body.

"I'd say this one is genuine. It's got your basic Austin tractor engine, which is pretty standard in these old Brit cars and the magnet stuck to the body. So we know it's steel and not a fiberglass replica. Let me check out the Chevy, though."

I began to work on the '57 Chevy. I checked the engine number and examined the fuel injector setup. Wiping my hands on a rag, I began pouring over one of the books I'd brought along.

"Well, doctor. How is the patient?" asked Morrison.

"It appears to be a real '57 Chevy ragtop but it's not all factory original. The serial number plate shows the car came from the factory as fuel injected all right, but the injector unit itself is off of a later model car."

"So it is counterfeit?"

"Well, it all depends how you look at it. We've actually entered a kind of a gray area here. See, when you're restoring something real old like this, the odds are that you won't be able to find the actual part that came on the car from the factory. It's considered ok to switch certain accessories as long as you use the same part from a different car. In other words, it's alright to use another fuel injector unit as long as it came from another '57 Chev. This one, however, is off of a Chevy from the mid 1960's. A '64 'Vette, to be exact. I wouldn't have thought a pro would make an error like that. I suppose it could happen, though. I'll give you a better diagnosis after I look at the rest."

I performed the same exam on the Shelby. A frown on my face apparently told the detective something wasn't quite right here, either.

"Yeah, this time the whole engine is wrong. This a standard 302 cubic inch V8 out of a regular family car. Shelby's came with the high performance version of the 289 V8. Either someone blew the original motor and replaced it with this one or this was a standard Mustang 2+2 converted to look like a Shelby. Figuring that out will take doing some homework when I get back to South Mountain."

I moved on to the Barracuda. Again I went over it from bumper to bumper. This time I emerged from under the hood shaking my head.

"I don't understand this one at all. It looks real. I mean, sure, I know they only made a few of these things. But, again, the VIN plate says it's a hemi car and there is a hemi under the hood. But I can't match the engine number with anything in the book."

"Are you sure you checked everything? Could the factory have accidentally put a Chrysler or Dodge motor in it instead of a Plymouth one? I remember a few years ago General Motors slipped a few Chevy motors into some Oldsmobiles."

"No, I already thought of that. I just can't figure it out. There sits a hemi. Why doesn't it show up anywhere in the books?"

"Could it have been switched for one of a different year like the fuel injector unit on that Chevy?"

"I thought of that, too. I looked at all of them from 1964 on up until they quit building the thing. But.........hang on a minute; you might just have a point there after all. I'm only assuming that this is a 426 cubic inch engine. Back in the fifties, Chrysler used to make an earlier, small displacement version of the same basic engine.

They pretty much look the same at first glance. Let me do some more checking."

I went back to the book with a vengeance. My fingers literally flew as I flipped through page after page. All of a sudden I stopped and stabbed my finger at the middle of the page.

"There it is, I've found it!" I proclaimed.

"Ok," said Morrison. "So, where did it come from?"

"Are you ready for this? This baby once proudly resided under the hood of a 1956 Desoto."

"Hey, no kidding? I used to have one of those. Cool car. Push button shift.......anyway, what's it doing here, in a car fifteen years newer?"

"I can only guess, but here's how I see it. This was most likely a standard, cheap, everyday Barracuda. Whoever is faking these things probably got this old motor out of a junker for a hundred bucks or so and stuck it in here. You know, you can put almost any motor into any car if you know what you're doing. Anyway, after that, all you have to do is stick on the proper trim and decals. Print up a new serial number plate with the engine designation for a 426 hemi instead of whatever was originally in it, and you've got it made. See, as a plain jane Barracuda ragtop it's worth about twenty five grand in showroom condition. But with the hemi, the sky's the limit. These things can go for several hundred grand or more. If you figure they paid a couple grand for the car, a junkyard motor, and throw in a paint job, whoever these guys are, they're scoring big. Even though this is one of the old 331 cube hemis, the average person wouldn't be able to tell the difference by just a casual glance. They even changed the original generator to an alternator to make the job look real. They had me fooled. Course, they wouldn't fool Galen Govier, but I'm not in his class."

"Who's he?"

"He's the world expert on Mopar products. He can tell you everything about any Chrysler product ever built. The guy's a genius."

"Ok, so now we know these guys are as crooked as the day is long. Let's forget about the GTO; we can reasonably be sure it's a fake, too. Let's get to this million dollar Corvette. Tell me if it's the real McCoy, although I seriously doubt it."

I walked over to the Corvette. I circled it several times, looking at it from all angles. I lay down on the garage floor and shined my flashlight up under the front and rear fender wells. I checked out the differential, the gearbox, and steering box. Peering under the hood, I examined the engine for any numbers that I could find.

"Well, it's a fake, too. It should have a 377 cube engine with four Weber carbs. Now, I know Penske and several of the others who eventually ended up with these things after GM was done with them did switch motors. Most dropped 427s in them; easier to get parts for and still run away from the Cobras. So just having a different engine isn't a big deal in this case. However, this thing should have an aluminum differential and steering box. It doesn't. Also, the body should be paper thin fiberglass; almost transparent single layer. This is a standard thickness body. Now, it does have four wheel disc brakes like it's supposed to. But, the front rotors should be much larger. There's a lot of other discrepancies. No, this is a fake. And not a terribly good one, either. Whoever these guys are, they sure must be brazen if they tried to pass this thing off as a real Grand Sport."

"I guess they knew they could pull it off. They probably figured they had the general on the hook and could get that one big score. You have all the serial numbers written down and any other info you think you might need?" asked Morrison. "If so, let's get back on the road."

"Yeah, I've got what I need. Let's go."

Chapter 14

The phone rang for the fifth time before the detective was finally able to reach it after a run from the coffee bar down the hall to his office.

"Detective Sergeant Morrison, may I help you?"

"Dave, this is Gerry. I was right. That Shelby in the general's garage isn't a genuine GT-350 either. When I got home I called the Shelby Registry and checked the serial number through their computer data base. They keep track of each and every one ever built and can tell you in a minute where they're at and who owns them. I had the secretary punch it up on the computer and guess what? The particular car that was born with that serial number was totaled in a wreck at Road Atlanta race track in 1966 during the SCCA National Championships. Apparently someone else had access to those records. They must have simply made a new serial number plate with the wrecked cars number and stuck it on a regular Mustang fastback. Then all they had to do was buy a few Shelby emblems, Cobra valve covers, and a GT-350 steering wheel. Stick on all that stuff, yank out the back seat, and presto, instant Shelby."

"Far out. It's really that easy?"

"Easy enough to fool a novice like the general. He was a great military mind but a lousy car collector."

"Oh, by the way. I'm glad you called. I planned to call you this afternoon. I went through all the papers we brought back from the general's house. I've got all the ones dealing with his car collection separate. I figured you should see them. If you can back up the figures you quoted me, we've got at least major fraud on our hands. Can you come over Saturday?"

"You're going to be in on a Saturday? Ok, and I'll bring Bill. See you then."

Saturday morning saw Bill and I arrive at Morrison's office around 9 am.

"Ah, welcome fellows. Glad you could come, Bill. You'll probably be interested in some of these papers, too. There they are, guys. All the bills of sale are in there. Wait till you see some of those price tags" said Morrison as he pointed to a stack of papers in his 'Hold' basket.

Both of us began to examine the papers. I would take the top one, look it over, and then pass it on to Bill.

"Look at this one. Two hundred grand for that Shelby. That's way too much. No, I'll take that back. If it were authentic, it would be way too much. Since it's only a dressed up Mustang, it's highway robbery."

"Yeah, but check this one out." I held up the bill of sale for the Barracuda. "Go ahead, take a wild ass guess how much he paid for this baby."

"Oh, figuring the way he's been overpaying for everything else, I'd have to say probably a quarter of a million."

"That would be a good guess, at least under normal circumstances. In fact, that's about what it would sell for at Barrett Jackson. But the general paid quadruple that price."

"You're kidding? He paid a cool mil? That's insane."

"Yeah, but you and I know what it's really worth; he didn't. This is what happens when rookies think they can make a quick buck."

"Hey guys. While I think of it, let me ask you a question. I found this stuck in with that stack over there. Does it make any sense to you? I can't make heads or tails out of it" asked the detective.

He passed a yellow piece of paper to me. The words 'Wendals Garage' were printed across the top. The second line read 'General Repair'. Underneath that was an address listing in nearby Fayetteville. Scrawled across the middle of the page in blue ink were the words 'adjust 3 x 2 – rich'. At the bottom, in the same blue ink it read 'no charge' and 'Classic Investments'. I read it and passed the paper over to Bill.

"Well, do you two have any idea what it means?" asked Morrison.

"Sure. It's a receipt for work done on that GTO in the general's garage. You see, that particular car has three, two barrel carburetors. Apparently it wasn't running up to par when the general picked it up; too rich according to this receipt. It looks like Classic Investments brought it to this 'Wendals Garage' for a carb adjustment. Oh, by the way, he paid way too much for that car also."

"Why do you suppose they would have a receipt for that work, though? Since they're ripping off the general, don't you think they would have just adjusted the thing and returned it with no questions asked?"

"They probably figured it would look more legitimate with a receipt from a garage where the work was actually done. They also probably did the work way out here instead of closer the generals' home to keep suspicions down to a minimum" I said.

"What do you mean by that" asked Morrison.

"Remember, Dave" said Bill. "We're not talking about some four door Toyota here. A car like that GTO sticks out like a sore thumb. Since they're not exactly above board here, they most likely would like to keep things as hush hush as possible. And that means getting work done on their cars as far away from the new owners as possible."

"Exactly. Hey, we should go check out that garage. Want to go, Dave?"

"I doubt they're open on a Saturday afternoon. Besides, I've got some work to do on the murder angle. We're digging up some great fraud stuff, but remember, what got us into this whole thing was the general's murder. My boss is getting impatient for some kind of progress. Maybe we'll drive out there one day next week. See you two later."

With that, the detective returned to the papers on his desk. We assumed that meant our meeting was over so we went back to the car. After buckling in, I turned to Bill.

"Want to go check out Wendal and his garage?"

"Why not? Like the man said, they probably aren't open anyway. We can look around and then come back and check out the Fayetteville flea market."

With my GPS unit programmed, we easily found the road listed on the receipt Morrison had shown us. However, after driving up and down the narrow dirt road several times, we were no closer locating the garage than before. The only thing that looked remotely like a business establishment was an old deserted junk yard. Weeds grew up around the high tin panels haphazardly nailed onto some rotten old boards to form a kind of fence around the yard. The only way to see in was through the rusted gate that hung precariously by one hinge. I pulled up to the gate and, looking through, tried to find any sign of life on the other side. The only thing visible was a tumble down building that probably once served as an office and possibly a garage.

"Hey, see that sign, Gerr?" Bill pointed to a worn, barely visible sign over the door to the building. It read 'Wendal Pentz, Proprietor'. "Wendal, get it? This must be Wendals Garage. Hang on, I'll open the gate."

Bill got out and carefully held open the rusty gate while I drove through. After closing it, he returned to the car.

"This place might look deserted, but somebody's been here fairly recently. There's fresh tire tracks coming through that gate."

"Well, in that case I'll park around back so this thing won't be so noticeable."

"Good idea. A mint 'Vette would kind of stand out around this place."

I drove around behind the building and backed down between two rows of junk cars, effectively hiding the Corvette from view. We got out and carefully snuck down behind the rear of the run down building. The windows were boarded up, so there was no way for us to get a look inside. Bill tried the rear door but it was padlocked shut.

"What do we do now?" he asked.

"I think I can get us in" I replied. I reached into an inside pocket of the photographers vest I happened to be wearing and pulled out a slim leather case. From it, I selected two thin pieces of steel. I inserted both into the key slot of the padlock. I hadn't tried this in a while, but I was pretty sure I could still do it. Holding one in place, I jiggled the other one around while turning it clockwise. All of a sudden, the old lock popped open in my hand.

"After you, Bill."

"Oh, so now you're a talented lock pick, too. I suppose the Air Force taught you that in tech school?"

"No, actually I took a correspondence course in lock smithing several years back. I didn't have much to do at the time and I figured it might come in handy some day."

Bill pushed the rickety door inward and fumbled blindly for a light switch. Finally his hand came upon one and he switched it on. Bright fluorescent light flooded the inside of the building. Both of us blinked from the blinding light and then gasped in surprise at the sight before us. The inside of the building was the total opposite of the outside. The floor was tiled and spotlessly clean. The walls were paneled with equally spotless workbenches on one side. Above the benches, each tool hung in its place. One corner was walled off as if it were a paint booth. In the middle of the floor sat a 1969 Pontiac Tempest in gray primer. Stacked in the other corner were hoods, mag wheels, and other assorted body parts.

"Pretty fancy for a deserted garage, huh?" said Bill. "Do you think what I think is going on here?"

"Yep. Look over here on the bench. GTO emblems and Judge decals. This has got to be where the counterfeit cars are coming from. And right in our own back yard, so to speak. All they need is a straight body and a decent engine. Then give it a paint job and stick on the proper emblems. See, over there is a hood with all the right air scoops ready to turn this everyday Tempest into a GTO."

"Not a bad setup" replied Bill as he picked up one of the Judge decals and held it under the light for a better view. "Hey, listen. Did you hear something?"

I turned my head slightly. The sound of the rusty gate being dragged open was unmistakable. I ran to one of the windows and tried to peer through a crack between the boards. I could see the grill of a Mercedes Benz begin to enter the yard. A burly man in a brown overcoat, hat pulled down over his eyes, stood by the gate.

"Quick, hit the light. Somebody's coming. We've got to hide. I know, in the trunk of the Pontiac. Hurry!"

Bill climbed in first with me right behind. I pulled the trunk lid down and latched it. We lay there, side by side, daring not to breathe.

The rickety old door opened and closed. We could hear two sets of heavy footsteps on the tile floor. Both sets seemed to be walking towards the workbench.

"I thought I told you to make sure you locked the door the last time we were here?" said one of the men in a gruff voice.

"I did. As old as that lock is, it probably popped back open. You could spend a few bucks and buy a decent one" answered the other man defiantly.

"Yeah, yeah. I suppose you're in charge now, huh? Just open the damn briefcase and let's see the boss's handiwork this time."

We could hear briefcase locks snap open and papers being removed.

"What do you think they're doing out there?" whispered Bill.

"I don't know. Just shut up before we get caught" I whispered back.

"These are great. The boss has done it again. I can't tell these fake titles from the real thing. Let me see those VIN plates" said the first man. "Oh, yeah. They're perfect. It'd take a real pro to tell these from the genuine article. Put them in the cabinet and let's get out of here. I always get the feeling the roof's going to cave in any minute around this place. Besides, we've got other stops to make before we're done."

We could hear a file cabinet drawer being slid open and then closed. Definitely needs greased, I thought. The heavy footsteps retraced their original path and seconds later the door slammed shut. We could hear one of the men fumble with the lock, cursing heavily under his breath. I reached into another of my vest pockets and pulled out the small flashlight I habitually carried. Clicking it on, I surveyed the interior of the Pontiac's trunk. Playing it on the lock, I manipulated a small lever and the lid popped up slightly. Cautiously I lifted the trunk lid and looked out. Seeing no one, I climbed out and went to the window. Peering out through the same crack as before, I got there just in time to see the burly man closing the gate and the tail lights of the Mercedes leaving the junk yard.

"Hey, you know something. That guy looks like the security guard at the general's estate. No, it couldn't be. I guess all big ugly guys look the same. Oh, by the way, you can come out now; the coast is clear."

"Man, you are a genius with locks. I'd never have been able to open that trunk" said Bill as he climbed out.

"Oh, that was easy. Think about it for a minute. Trunks are like safes. They're designed to keep someone on the outside from getting in. They're not designed to keep someone on the inside from getting out. Now, let's go see what they put into the file cabinet."

I walked over to the end of the bench. I pulled one drawer, then another. They were all empty except for the top one.

"Look at this" I exclaimed. "Titles and VIN plates. Here's one for that Tempest. That is, it used to be a Tempest. Now it's a GTO Judge."

"Let's see what else they're planning to build" said Bill. He took the handful of titles and leafed through them. "Here's one for a Mach I Mustang, an SS 396 Chevelle, and a Road Runner. Well, like we said before, they do have very good taste in cars. At least they're faking the good stuff. Not a dog in the bunch, that is if you leave out the

Ford. Say, I wonder how much they're going to ask for the SS 396?"

"Right. You're knowingly going to buy a counterfeit car from a bunch of thieves. Where does your mind go on these little trips?"

"As long as I kept it for my own personal use and didn't try to pawn it off to someone as the real thing, it would be ok. Besides, I was only kidding. Let's get out of here before anyone else comes snooping around."

We put the papers back into the file and closed it. I went to the door and gave it a hard tug. To my surprise, it flew inward, almost knocking me off my feet.

"Guess they figured the hell with the lock" I muttered. Bill closed the door and we returned to the car.

"Go check out front and make sure nobody's coming up the road. If it's clear, give me the high sign and I'll bring the car around."

Bill slipped through the gate and cautiously peeked around the fence to the right. Seeing nothing, he looked left. Satisfied that the area was truly deserted, he waved me on. He swung open the gate and I idled the car forward. Closing it again, he jumped into the passenger seat just as the Corvette leaped forward.

"Now what do we do?" Bill asked.

"Well," I replied, looking at my watch. "It's already five thirty. I think it's probably too late to catch Morrison at the office so about the only thing we can do is go home and I'll call him later tonight."

Later that evening, I finally got through to the detective at his apartment. I told him of the trip to Wendals Garage and of hiding in the trunk when the two men had shown up.

"So, let me get this straight, you picked the lock and just walked in? Of course, you know that's called breaking and entering, right?"

"Well, it was a really old lock. And it really didn't work very well. And I'll disavow it all in court. Now, what are you going to do about those two guys?"

"What can I do, legally that is? I'll tell you, not much. I can't use your little escapade as justification for a search warrant. We just don't have any hard evidence to go before a judge with.

I realize you two are hot about these fake muscle cars but we really have to let someone else handle it. The general's murder still comes first. Besides, Fayetteville is out of my jurisdiction anyway. I work for Adams County, remember? Listen, I'm going to the National Achieves on Monday to review the general's military records; want to come along?"

"Sorry, no can do. I've got an article due in two days and I've really got to get on it. Bill might want to go, though; why don't you give him a ring?"

"You know, that's not a bad idea. I realize he wasn't in the military but I imagine his experience in the fire department might be helpful as well."

Chapter 15

The sun was just peaking over the horizon when Bill wheeled his for four wheel drive pickup truck into the sheriff departments' parking lot. He's probably not here yet, thought Bill. Maybe I'll have time to run over to that donut shop.

At that very moment, Morrison's brown four door sedan bounced into the lot and pulled up beside Bills truck.

"Want to grab a couple of donuts and a cup of java before we leave?" asked the detective, rolling down his window.

"Man, you must be reading my mind. I was just thinking about doing that. Let's go."

After quaffing down two donuts each and a steaming cup of coffee, they both piled into the detectives car for the ride to Washington. Morrison arrived on the DC beltway an hour and a half later. He then followed Interstate 395 northward into the downtown area.

"Ok, Bill. You're taking over Gerry's place as navigator. How do I get to the National Archive building?"

"No Problem. I know my way around DC like the back of my hand. Turn left at the next street. Good, now just go straight for a block or two. There, see that building over there?" Bill pointed to a large building on the right side of the next intersection. "That's the National Art Gallery. It's part of the Smithsonian. Right behind it is the National Achieves. Find a place to park and we're there."

Just as he finished speaking, a car pulled out of a parking space next to the Art Gallery. Morrison signaled and then deftly backed into the vacated space.

"Not bad, for a cop" Bill joked as he locked the car door.

"And I can catch you on a back road if you try to out run me, too" replied the detective. "Come on, let's get to work."

The warm sun reflected off the spotless marble staircase as they climbed the steps and entered into the foyer. Morrison walked up to the information desk and rang the shiny little bell on the counter. A petite black woman in her mid twenties emerged from around a corner to answer their inquiry.

"Hello, may I help you gentlemen?" she asked in a melodic voice.

"You may. I'm Detective Sergeant Morrison of Adams County, Pennsylvania. This is one of my consultants, Mr. South. We're investigating the murder of Air Force General Wilford Malcomb. We would like to review the general's service record and anything else you might be able to offer."

Morrison flipped open his leather case to reveal his gold badge as he spoke. The girl gave it a cursory look and placed a piece of paper, along with a ball point pen in from of the detective.

"Fill out this form and take it to the representative in Section 15B. Just go past the guard and through the metal detector." She gestured towards a contraption just like those found in airports. Morrison showed his gold shield to the guard, removed his gun, and walked through. When Bills turn came, he emptied his pockets and removed his belt buckle.

"You going to take off your pants, too?" asked Morrison innocently.

"No, smart ass. I've gone through so many of these things I know what'll set them off. And this chunk of metal keeping my belt together will do it every time."

"Well, if you weren't using a Mercedes Benz hubcap for a belt buckle, you wouldn't have that problem" laughed the detective.

Holding his pants from falling down around his ankles, Bill walked through the metal detector. Upon reaching the other side, he reassembled his belt and refilled his pockets.

"Fifty thousand comedians out of work and you're trying to break into the business. Are you ready?" he replied as he tucked the tip of his belt through the first belt loop.

Morrison led the way down the aisle. Spotting a sign overhead pointing to Section 15, he made a quick turn between two bookshelves and almost ran over another young black woman.

"Oh, excuse me. I'm sorry. I wasn't looking where I was going. My friend and I are trying to find Section 15B so we can examine some old military records. Do you think you could point us in the right direction?"

"You came to the right place. It just so happens to be in my area. I look after section 10 through 15. Let me see your request form and we'll see what we can do for you."

Morrison handed over the form he had filled out at the front desk. The girl looked it over and motioned for the guys to follow her. She led them down the aisle, turned several corners, and finally entered a small, out of the way room.

"Here we are, gentlemen. Either of you know to operate a microfiche machine?"

"I do" answered Bill. "We used them to look up parts at a place I used to work."

"Good. Now, all military records are put on microfiche and stored here in these cabinets. They're all arranged alphabetically, of course. All you have to do is look in the 'M' cabinet and locate your general. Sorry, they're not computerized yet. May I assume he was on active duty for quite some time?"

"Right. He was a thirty year man" replied Morrison. "Why do you ask?"

"Just so I could get some idea of how long you'll be here. With that long a career, you'd better plan on being here the best part of the day. A guy collects an awful lot of paperwork in thirty years."

"Oh, yeah. I never thought of that. I guess we'd better get started. Bill, see if you can find the file, will you?"

The girl began to leave but turned to address the detective.

"If you need any help, feel free to give me a call. Oh, and if you want, you can copy any of the records. The machine has a built in printer. I'm sure your friend knows how to run it. Happy hunting."

With that, she turned and walked off. Morrison was still watching her shapely behind gently swaying from side to side when Bill returned with the file on General Wilford Malcomb.

"Come on, get your mind back on the business at hand, detective. There's a hell of a lot of microfiche here to look at."

"I know, but she's a much prettier sight than that stack of film you've got there."

Bill flipped on the microfiche viewer and inserted the first slide. General Macomb's very first enlistment contract popped up on the screen.

"My god, I see what she meant. This is going to be an all day job" said Bill as he scanned several more documents. "There's every piece of paper the Air Force collected for thirty years in here. How about I speed up the first few years?"

"Fine with me. Take us to the Vietnam era. I don't think we'll find much of interest this early in his career."

Bill quickly scanned through the microfiche. When he began seeing documents dated in the 1965 time frame, he slowed down and both men read each one carefully.

"Hey, check this one out. Here's one from the OSI opening an investigation on some chick. Let's see what they found."

Bill moved to the next frame. Instead of finding an answer to the question, they were both shocked to see the words 'Records Sealed' marked boldly across the screen. He moved to the next one. And the next. The rest of that film read the same.

"What the hell's going on? How come all these records are sealed?" asked Bill.

"Well, first you could tell me what OSI stands for. Remember, I haven't got a clue what all those military acronyms are all about."

"Oh, right. Sorry Dave. Office of Special Investigations."

"Sort of like the military version of the FBI? That's just great. Back then they could have been investigating anything. Maybe they thought this broad was a spy. Hell, maybe she was a spy. Of course, we'll never know now. Let's move along."

Bill removed the slide and inserted the next one. They looked through half of the next slide without finding anything interesting. Most of the slide appeared to be flight orders and the occasional temporary duty order.

"Here's a golden oldie, Dave. The generals request for permission to get married. Of course they don't have to play that silly game nowadays."

"You mean they used to have to get somebody's permission to get married?" asked Morrison incredulously.

"Yeah, back in the old days. Especially overseas. The idea was, if the military wanted you to have a wife, they'd have issued you one. But, actually, the brass wanted to make sure you were marrying someone they thought was worthy. Besides, they didn't want some guy to marry a commie spy or a hooker. Let's see, this must be for the present Mrs. Malcomb. I assume he was only married once, seeing how back then divorced guys just didn't make general."

"Right. Her maiden name was Sun Lee Chui. Hey, hang on a minute. What was the name of that girl the OSI was investigating? Quick, go back to the last slide."

Bill removed the current slide and placed the previous one back into the viewer. He moved the film back and forth under the lens until he found the letter in question.

"That's it! Sun Lee Chui! She's the one the OSI investigated. Now I'd really like to know what's in those sealed records."

"Well, it's a cinch we're not going to find out. Dave, when they seal these things, even the Freedom of Information Act won't get them open."

"So maybe we can get around it. Suppose we write down the names of some of the guys the general knew and hung out with back then and try to dig them up. They might have heard some rumors, hell, they might even know her."

"I guess it's worth a try. I'll make copies of some of these documents and then we can get on with it."

Bill lined up a document and pushed the square green button on the side of the viewer. Five seconds later, a perfect copy fell into the tray. He kept copying until the document tray was full.

"That ought to be enough to get us into trouble. You ready to go?"

"Yeah, let's put this stuff back where we found it and hit the road."

Bill returned the microfiche to the file he'd gotten it from and after checking out at the front desk, both men left the building. Following Bills directions, Morrison got them back out of the city and onto the beltway headed home.

Chapter 16

"Hey, Gerr, how's it going?" Bill flopped down in the empty easy chair beside my desk. "Ready to find out where these guys are now?"

"Yep, let's call the Locator and see if they can tell us anything."

Upon returning to Gettysburg, Bill had taken the list of the generals close associates in Vietnam home with him. He knew I had access to the Air Force Worldwide Personnel Locator at Randolph Air Force Base in San Antonio. We both felt that if there was a chance of finding anyone who had known the general over forty years ago, this would be our best shot.

"Hand me that phone book, will you? Thanks. Let's see. Peterson Air Force Base. Plattsburgh, Pope, Randolph. Here it is. You read off the number while I dial."

"Ready? 210-658-1110" Bill read.

I pushed the buttons and listened while the phone rang on the other end. On the third ring, a female voice with an unmistakable Texas drawl answered.

"Hello" I replied. "Could I have the number for the Worldwide Locator? Yes, that's right. Ok, 658-4120? Good, thank you very much. Bye."

I hung up the receiver for a second and then lifted it again. I dialed the number and waited for it to ring.

"Locator, Chief Lucas. May I help you?" said the voice on the other end of the phone.

"I sure hope so" I replied. "This is Gerry Campbell, retired Master Sergeant. I need to try and locate several individuals who used to be in the Air Force."

"I'm sorry, sarge. We're not allowed to give any info out over the phone. If you want to locate someone, you'll have to send a letter with a self addressed, stamped envelope for each name you want researched."

"Oh, I didn't realize that. My buddy and I are helping the police investigate the murder of an Air Force officer and we thought if we could find some of his old buddies, we could possibly get some helpful info from them."

"You wouldn't be referring to General Wilford Malcomb, would you?" asked the Chief Master Sergeant.

"Why, yes, actually. Did you know him?" I asked.

"I used to work on his wing mans F-4 in 'Nam before I cross trained into admin. Are you guys really trying to catch the bastard who killed him?"

"Yes sir, we're helping a local detective. He's using us as a kind of consultant on military affairs. In other words, he needs us to cut through the Air Force red tape."

"Well, sarge, this is your lucky day. This one's for the general. Just give me that list of names and we'll put this big old computer to good use."

"Thanks, Chief. Here we go. Second Lieutenant Leandro Gomez, Second Lieutenant Manfred Shoemaker, First Lieutenant Donald Pentz, Captain Michael Edwards, and Captain Bradley Hill. Think your fancy machine can find them?"

"Hell, I can tell you where Pentz is. He was Macomb's wing man. Remember I told you I worked on his plane? Donnie and I still keep in touch, only now he's a Colonel flying C-141s out of Andrews Air Force Base. Hang on, I'll tell you in a minute where the others are."

I waited on the other end of the phone while the master computer checked through its data base of hundreds of thousands of active and former Air Force members. I could hear the Chief pushing buttons and writing on a pad at the other end of the line.

"Got your info, sarge. Like I told you, Pentz is at Andrews. Unfortunately Gomez is dead. Shot down over 'Nam in '71. Shoemaker is at Yokota Air Base in Japan. Hill retired last year to somewhere in northern Canada; all I have is a post office box. Edwards is doing a joint assignment with the army at the War College in Carlisle, Pennsylvania. He's also a Colonel. Does that help you guys out?"

"You bet, Chief. Two of these gentlemen are close enough that we can drive over and question them in person. We can't thank you enough for your help."

"Sarge, just catch that bastard for me. That's all the thanks I need. Got to get back to work now. Good hunting." With that, he hung up the phone.

"Well, we've got a little something to go on. Two of these guys are fairly close. Pentz is down at Andrews and Edwards is in Carlisle. Which one should we tackle first?"

"How about Carlisle? We can take our golf clubs and play a round after we interview this guy."

"That's not a bad idea. There aren't going to be too many nice days left. I'd better call him first, though. He works at the War College and he might be teaching class all day."

The Army War College taught selected military, civilian, and international leaders the use of land power in warfare. The War College currently resided on the site originally occupied by the Carlisle Indian Industrial School. The schools most famous graduate was the world renowned Jim Thorpe. Thorpe was coached in football at the school by the legendary 'Pop' Warner. The War College gymnasium was named for Thorpe.

I brought up the college web site on my laptop and found the schools phone number. I quickly dialed it and when the operator answered, I asked for Colonel Edwards's number.

"History Department, Colonel Edwards. May I help you?"

"Yes, sir" I replied. This is retired Master Sergeant Gerry Campbell. An associate and I are helping a Pennsylvania detective investigate the murder of General Wilford Malcomb. We understand you knew him in Vietnam. We'd like to ask you a few questions if you don't mind. Would that be possible?"

"Of course. I'd heard about Wills death. Tragic. I'd be happy to help out. Where would you like to meet? There's a great little Mexican joint just outside the main gate. I highly recommend it, that is, unless you don't like Mexican food."

"Oh, that's just fine with us, Colonel. Well, actually it does do strange things to Bills insides but that's ok. Let's see, it's one thirty now, how about we meet you there at three?"

"I'll see you then, Sergeant" replied the Colonel.

Chapter 17

A little over an hour later I wheeled the Corvette into the parking lot of the Los Amigos Mexican Villa. The small, low white building glistened in the afternoon sun. Generations of GIs had quenched their thirst inside this inviting little eatery. We walked in and made our way to the bar. Happy mariachi music filled the air, courtesy of the old fashioned juke box in the far corner. Several soldiers shared a table overlooking the pool table while two of their members shot a game of nine ball. Various army unit emblems adorned the walls with an occasional air force one thrown in. We picked two stools close to the front door.

"What'll you boys have?" asked the bartender. A short, elderly gentleman, he wore a green visor on his forehead that made him look more like a bookie than a bar keep.

"I'll have a Sam Adams, how 'bout you, Bill? Still drinking the rot gut?" I laughed.

"Very funny. Make mine a Bud Lite. Got to watch my youthful figure, you know."

"Yeah, right. Youthful and figure are a contradiction in terms in your case."

I laid a five dollar bill on the bar and took my first sip of ice cold beer when the front door flew open. A tall man entered wearing Air Force blue. The silver eagles on his epaulets identified him as a full colonel and the ultramarine blue name tag over his right pocket proclaimed his surname to be Edwards.

"You two must be the detectives who wish to question me" he said to them with a twinkle in his eye.

"Yes sir. After you get your drink why don't we move to a table where we'll be a little more comfortable?"

"Capital idea, my boy. Oh, publican, may I have a Guinness?" the Colonel exclaimed.

The short bartender brought a brown bottle and placed it in front of the Colonel. He handed several bills to the bartender and picked up the bottle of stout.

"Shall we move, then, gentlemen?"

With that, all three of us rose from our stools and found a dimly lit table by the back wall.

"I'll take it you were stationed in the United Kingdom, Colonel" I said as I pulled in my chair.

"You're quite right, detective. How can you tell?"

"Well, sir. First of all, you're drinking stout. And then you called the bartender 'Publican'. I deduced from that you'd been in the UK."

"Very good. But how do you know I wasn't in Australia instead? It could be, you know."

"Oh, that's easy, Colonel. I was stationed in Australia and they don't call for the 'Publican' over there. They just yell 'Ey, bring me a bloody beer, mate" I laughed.

"Ok, you've got me there" laughed the Colonel in return. "Now, what can I do for you?"

"Tell us a little about General Malcomb. What do you remember most about him? What kind of guy was he? What was his wife like?"

"Well, let me think. He was a hell of a pilot, I remember that. He always took good care of his ground crew, too. If they kept his plane flying, he'd bring them each a bottle of good booze every so often. They really loved him for that."

"What do you remember about his wife, Colonel?"

Just as he opened his mouth to answer, a waitress appeared beside their table.

"Can I get y'all somethin', fellas?"

"My, you don't exactly sound Mexican, young lady."

"No, sir. I'm originally from LA."

"You certainly don't sound like you're from Los Angeles, either" I said.

"No, silly. Lower Arkansas. Now, can I get y'all something or not?"

"I think I'll just have a couple of tacos; how about you guys?"

"I believe I'll have the same. Colonel?"

"Sounds good to me. Tacos all around."

The pretty waitress thanked us and walked away.

"Ok, back to Wills' wife. The thing that most stands out in my memory is her talent. She was an outstanding artist. Not just a painting artist. She was a very talented engraver. I remember there was a rumor going around that she was involved in something underhanded but I never believed it, really. She was just too sweet and innocent to be involved in anything even a bit shady. She's supposed to be related to royalty, you know."

"So we've heard. Did you ever hear any rumors about the general? I mean, any get rich quick schemes or anything like that? I was in 'Nam, so I know what young GIs are like."

"Then, Sarge, you ought to know there were all sorts of rumors about almost everybody over there. You know what I mean. Drug dealing, black market, white slavers, the whole nine yards. I never heard anything about Will, though. You ought to find some of the other guys we ran around with. They might be about to help you more. I'm afraid that's all I know."

"We plan to talk face to face with at least one more of the general's buddies. We'll probably call a couple more on the phone as well. Oh, looks like lunch is served."

Chapter 18

Bright and early Saturday morning I pulled into Bills driveway. Normally I'd blow the horn to get Bills attention but since it was so early, I decided to just ring the door bell instead. No need to wake the whole neighborhood, I figured.

Bill and his wife live about half a mile from me. It's one of those picture perfect little cottages with the white picket fence. A perfectly groomed hedge surrounded the entire yard. Geraniums bloomed a brilliant red on either side of the front door. Beds under each window were filled to overflowing with assorted flowers of all colors. Lovely rose bushes lined the driveway. Of course, none of this was due to Bill. Everything he planted died within the week. It was his wife that had the green thumb in the family.

I surveyed the sea of color as I rang the bell and waited for an answer. She's good, I thought. I wondered if she'd like to work her magic over at my place. My train of thought was suddenly interrupted by the door opening.

"Hi, Gerr. I'll be ready in just a minute. Come on in and have a cup of coffee."

"Ok" I replied as I closed the door behind me. "How would Betty like a real challenge? Think she could do for my place what she's done for this one?"

"That woman could make hair grow on a bowling ball. She drives me crazy. But I don't know if even she could make anything grow in that concrete you call dirt."

"Hey, that's good mountain ground."

"Sure it is. You just have to blast if you want to grow anything in it. Listen, I'll be right back; gotta finish shaving. Help yourself to the coffee" replied Bill as he turned back the hallway towards the bathroom.

I went over to the kitchen counter and opened the overhead cabinet. I chose a mug and filled it with steaming coffee and added just a pinch of sugar. Returning to the living room, I threw myself down on the couch.

"Hurry up, will you? I'd like to get there before the place gets too crowded."

"I'm coming, I'm coming. You sure you've got enough gunpowder? I remember last time."

"Yes, I made sure of it. Ah, finally. Let's go."

Bill walked into the living room followed by a blond haired, blue eyed vision of beauty in a lovely pink nightgown. She was tall but not too tall.

"Hi, Betty. I didn't wake you, I hope."

"No, I was already up. Bill couldn't get out of bed quietly if his life depended on it. You won't let him shoot his foot off, will you?"

"I promise. We're only going to sight in the guns for deer season. Which reminds me, let's get going before hunting season is over."

"It doesn't start for a month or so. See you, babe. We won't be too long" said Bill as he kissed his wife lovingly on the cheek.

He picked up his Kentucky long rifle from beside the front door where he'd stood it earlier that morning. Waving to Betty, he pulled the door closed behind him.

"Grab your rifle, old buddy. Throw it in the truck and we're off."

I retrieved my own rifle from the Corvette and slid it behind the seat of Bills Chevy pickup. Bill backed out of the driveway and pulled the steering column mounted shifter down into first gear. Letting out the clutch, we were off.

He drove to the end of the road and then, after stopping, went straight across the intersection. After a short while, the road turned to dirt. Bill drove for half a mile and turned onto another dirt road. Upon arriving at a yellow gate, I alighted from the truck and using a special key, opened the gate. I pushed it open enough for the truck to get through and then closed and locked it again.

"Almost there, old buddy. We'll be knocking the bull's eye out of those targets in no time."

He spun the steering wheel to the left, skidding the rear of the truck around on the dirt road. The Chevy bounced to a stop in the makeshift parking lot.

"Well, we did it! First ones here! Let's get the targets" I said.

We gathered all of our equipment and walked into the range. This trek had become an annual event for us. At a predetermined time before the first day of deer hunting season every year, we took our muzzle loading rifles out to sight them in.

The range we frequent belongs to the local fish and game club where we both are members. The range is about twenty years old but just had a new addition added last year. There are places for targets to be set at 25, 50, 100, and 200 yards.

With targets set at 100 yards, both of us set about preparing our rifles. First the powder was poured down the barrel. A cotton patch followed, topped off with a round lead ball. The combination was pushed all the way to the breech with a fiberglass ramrod. A percussion cap was placed on the nipple and the hammer pulled fully rearward.

"Ready when you are, Gerr."

"Go for it. Let's fire three rounds to establish a grouping. Bet you a beer I shoot a tighter group."

"You're on" replied Bill.

Both of us put on ear protectors and shooting glasses. We took careful aim and fired. Orange flame and arid white smoke exploded from the muzzle of each rifle. We reloaded and fired twice more. Each time the hammers fell, the rifles belched flame and smoke.

"It's good we only fire three" Bill said. "I don't think I would have been able to see the target for all the smoke if we kept going. Let's go check my winning target."

"You haven't won yet, my friend. I still say I'm a better shot than you" I replied.

We walked the hundred yards to the far end of the range. We examined Bills target first. One hole was in the lower left corner of the bull's eye, while the other two holes were in the next ring or the 'nine' ring as it is commonly called.

"Not bad shooting, Bill. 'Course now we go check the winner."

"You know you can't beat that. Why not save yourself the embarrassment and concede now?" Bill laughed.

"Ah, I'll have a Sam Adams, if you don't mind" I answered, holding up my target. Two holes were barely in the bull's eye, the other in the nine ring. "Looks like you lose again."

"I don't believe it. Again? That's, what, ten years running?"

"Eleven, but who's counting? Ready to go again?"

"Might as well. Make sure you put tape over those holes. I don't want you cheating on me."

"Consider it done."

We went back to the bench rests and began to reload our rifles. Absentmindedly I glanced over at Bill while I was reloading my rifle. Bill had just put the bullet into the muzzle using the short ball starter and was reaching for the ramrod to push it the rest of the way home when I let out a yell!

"That's it! I know who did it! Well, not exactly who, but I know how we can find out" I yelled excitedly.

"Hey, hey. Slow down. What do you mean you know how we can find out? Find out what?"

"I know how we can find out who killed the general. It just came to me. Think about it for a minute; to kill someone with a muzzle loader, you have to use a bullet, right?"

"Well, obviously, Dr. Einstein. So?"

"So, to use a bullet, you have to get it down the barrel. To get it down the barrel, you have to use a ramrod. You know when we do reenactments we're prohibited from using the ramrod because of potential accidents. Whoever killed the general had to seat the bullet. All we have to do is watch those tapes again and locate the guy who uses a ramrod and we have the killer."

"Wow, you're right! Everybody else on the tape will be just pouring gun powder down the barrel. The killer ought to stick out like a sore thumb. Damn, we should have thought of that sooner."

"Yeah, you're right. We sure should have. Let's go tell Morrison."

After dropping off our rifles and showering, we both climbed into the 'Vette and drove east to Gettysburg. In half an hour's time I had parked the car and we were in the court house basement. We'd been there so often recently that we knew exactly where to find the detective. I burst into his office with Bill following tight on my heals.

"Dave, we've got it! We know how to find the killer!" I exclaimed.

"Great, who is it?"

"Well, we don't actually know his name" replied Bill. "Or what he looks like."

"Then how am I supposed to arrest him? You just told me you guys know who he is?"

"No, what we said was, we know how to find him. Look, Dave, get those video tapes of the reenactment out and we'll show you what we mean."

"All right, let's go down to the video studio and maybe you'll clue me in as to what you two are talking about."

It took a couple of minutes for their eyes to adjust to the dimly lit studio. Morrison went directly to the VHS video equipment and powered it up. Selecting the first tape, he inserted it and pushed the play button.

"Ok, guys. What's the deal?"

"Dave, do you remember the day of the murder? Remember I let you load and shoot my rifle?"

"Sure, why?"

"That time we were only using gunpowder. All you did was pour the powder down the barrel and fire. Remember I told you during reenactments we are not allowed to use ramrods because of safety regulations? Well, the only way to actually shoot a bullet out of a muzzle loader is to seat it all the way down the barrel with the ramrod. So, all we have to do is watch the tapes and find the one guy who will be using his ramrod and we'll have the killer. Understand?"

"Oh, hell yeah! I get it! Whoever it is ought to stick out like a sore thumb! Great thinking, guys! Pull up a chair and make yourself at home; it'll be another long day!"

Again all three of us watched tape after tape. Finally half way through the third tape, I jumped to my feet.

"There he is! Right there, see him?" I pointed.

Excitedly I pointed to a gray clad soldier. The man wore a fairly standard Confederate uniform with a gray slouch hat pulled way down, hiding his face. He was just returning the rifles ramrod to its holder under the barrel when I spotted him.

Morrison pushed the 'Stop' button on the VCR and rewound the tape a foot or two. He pushed 'Play' and we watched the scene unfold before us again. The long gray line surged towards the column of Yankee blue. The camera operator apparently wanted to get as complete a picture as possible because he or she had kept the camera lens open at a rather wide angle. Again we watched the suspect fire, stop, and then pour powder from a paper cartridge into the rifles barrel. He then appeared to slip something else into the muzzle and then pulled the ramrod from under the barrel. He inserted it and pushed all the way to the breech. The man quickly withdrew it

144

and reinserted it into its holder. All three of us watched in horror as he took very deliberate aim and fired. On the far right hand side of the screen we saw the general's body double over and fall.

"Well, that's it. There's the murder right in front of our eyes. What do we do now?" I asked.

"I'd suggest marking this spot and then watching the rest of the tapes to see if we get any different angles. Either of you have a pencil?"

Bill offered the detective ball a point pen instead. Taking it, he wrote down the numbers showing on the VCRs digital counter. Now, he explained, we'll be able to find this exact spot again very easily.

The final tape and a half didn't reveal anything else we could use. The mystery man appeared briefly but was so obscured by other soldiers the scene was of little or no use to us.

"Back to tape three, fellows. I guess that's our only shot of the guy. I just wish we could get a better look at his face" I said.

"Ah, but you haven't seen all the marvels of modern technology. Watch that computer screen over there" answered the detective.

He advanced the tape forward frame by frame until he felt he had the best view of the suspect. Then, after flipping a few switches, the same picture appeared on a different computer screen across the room.

"Now we can try to enhance this frame, and with a little luck, we'll be able to ID the bastard."

We crossed the room and Morrison sat down facing the screen. Working the keyboard with well practiced skill, he zoomed in on the suspect. Satisfied that he had the best picture possible, he hit a few more keystrokes and the laser printer sitting next to the computer began to hum. Within half a minute, a completed page ejected from the printer and landed into the bin beneath it.

"What do you think now?" Morrison asked, holding the finished picture up for us to see.

"Pretty damn good; I'm impressed. I suppose we have the Japanese to thank for that marvelous little bit of technology?" replied Bill.

"No, actually I think that's one of ours. Surprising, isn't it? The computer digitizes and enhances the picture. It's fairly new technology; we've only had ours a month or two and this is the first big time case it's been used on. That's your tax dollars at work, boys."

"You know" I said. "I'm sure I've seen that guy before. I just can't place him. You ever see him, Bill?"

"I'm not really sure. With that hat pulled down so low, I can't get a good look. He does look familiar, though. How about you, Dave?"

"Sorry, the best I can do is go through the mug books and hope he shows up somewhere. Problem is, with half his face obscured like that, it could be almost any garden variety hood."

"You know, that's it!" I exclaimed. "You just said it! He looks like a hood! He reminds me of the one guy from that deserted garage we went to the other day. Remember him, Bill?"

"Hey, come on, Gerr. I was in the trunk of the Pontiac, remember? I couldn't see a thing."

"Oh, yeah. I forgot. Well, anyway, I'd swear that's the same guy. Stocky, hat pulled down like that. Same jaw. I'd almost bet on it."

Chapter 19

"Colonel Pentz, please. Yes, I'll hold. Who's this? Oh, this is retired Master Sergeant Campbell."

"Well, are we going to be able to talk to him?" asked Bill.

"I think so. His secretary is going for him. I'm on hold right now" I replied. "Why don't you grab the extension so you can listen in?"

"Good idea" answered Bill as he picked up my extension from the kitchen.

Finally a voice came onto the other end of the phone.

"Hello, this is Colonel Pentz. Master Sergeant Campbell? What can I do for you?"

"Sir, my friend and I are assisting a local detective to investigate the death of General Wilford Malcomb. We understand you knew him in Vietnam. We'd appreciate any information you could give us about either the general or his wife that might help us out. You know, what kind of guy he was, did he have many friends, that sort of thing."

"Oh, I'll tell you, Sergeant, I was just shocked when I heard about Will's death. I don't understand how an accident like that could happen. I was his wingman, you know."

"Yes sir, we know. What kind of officer was he in his younger days, Colonel?"

"Oh, he was the typical fighter jock, I suppose. Kind of wild, kind of cocky. Took lots of chances on the ground but never in the air. Hell of a pilot, that Will. Why, I remember one time we were outnumbered two to one over the DMZ. He shot down three MIGs before they put a cannon round in his tail. He nursed that F-4 all the way back to the airfield and still smoked another MIG on the way. I've never seen anything like it. Got the Air Medal for that. Yes, sir, one hell of a pilot."

"How about his wife; what was she like?"

"That's funny you should mention her. The OSI came around investigating her when Will decided to get married. At first I didn't think too much about it, but some of the questions they asked, well I started to wonder."

"What kinds of questions?" I asked, glancing over at Bill.

"Well, they wanted to know if she was loyal to South Vietnam or if we knew of any sympathy for the Viet Cong. They asked a lot about where she got her money, too."

"So where *did* she get her money, Colonel?"

"All I know is she always told us she was related to the royal family. She never was the typical bar girl. That's where he met her, by the way. A bar in Saigon. Always seemed too smart, too cunning. Old Will, he fell for her hook, line, and sinker. I never trusted her, though. You know what I mean; she acted like the doting little wife, but there was that nagging feeling that she was doing all the manipulating."

"Was there any suspicion of illegal activities, that you know of, sir?"

This time the colonel lowered his voice as he spoke.

"I heard of all sorts of scuttlebutt through the grapevine, but of course that kind of thing went on about almost everybody over there who happened to have some unexplained cash. Thing is, Will's wife was an artist. Rumors had her copying great masterpieces, forging passports, laundering money for the Japanese mobs, and even drug smuggling. They never proved anything but one day I was over at their house and I could swear Will had Van Gogh's 'Sunflowers' on his bedroom wall. I asked him about it and he told me it was a poor copy his wife had painted. A couple days later when I stopped in for a beer, it was gone. Shortly after that she bought a brand new Citroen SM. Really cool car. Maserati engine. Hydraulic suspension. But I digress. Anyway, all that probably doesn't mean anything because I can't prove she did anything wrong and neither could anyone else. But I'd almost bet my next paycheck that she painted an exact copy and shipped it abroad. Sold it to some anonymous collector for a handsome sum, no doubt. That's probably what bought her new car. Then again, like I told you, I never really trusted her so I might be making a mountain out of a molehill."

His voice was almost a whisper now. To me it seemed as if the Colonel was still trying to rationalize his feelings after four decades.

"Colonel, we realize you're a busy man so we won't take up any more of your valuable time. We certainly appreciate the information you've given us and I promise as soon as we find General Macomb's killer, you'll be one of the first to know. Again, many thanks, sir."

"Only too glad to help, Sergeant. If you need anything else, let me know."

"Yes sir, thank you. We'll do that."

I hung up the phone and turned to Bill.

"What do you think? Not one of her biggest fans, is he?"

"Definitely not. But like he said, none of it can ever be proven. Besides, it was probably nothing. She just threw the picture out because she didn't like it; figured it was a lousy copy and she could do better next time."

"I guess you might be right. A twenty two year old college kid back then had lots of wild ideas and saw almost everything as a conspiracy of some sort. Or maybe she started a counterfeiting career at an early age. Think we should call our detective friend and let him in on the good colonels' suspicions?"

"Yeah, but let's wait until after lunch, I'm starved" I replied. Did you bring anything along to eat?"

"No, I figured you'd want some hot dogs with everything from Ernie's. Best in town, remember?"

"Ok, now you've got my mouth watering. Let's go!"

Chapter 20

Dave Morrison paid for the pizza and turned to leave the shop. Not being able to resist the tantalizing aroma, he lifted the lid to smell the wonderful mixture of cheese, onions, mushrooms, green peppers, and tomato sauce. Ah, he thought to himself, nobody in this town makes a pizza quite like Rocky. Throw in a cold six pack and I'll be in seventh heaven. If I've got it figured just right, the Steelers and Ravens should be kicking off just about the time I pour the first icy brew.

He opened the door of the shop and walked out into the night. It was dark now, but fortunately he had parked under a street lamp. Looking both ways, he stepped into the street. At the end of the block, an automobile engine started. Headlights suddenly blinded him. Balancing the pizza in his left hand, he shaded his eyes with the right. With rubber burning, the car leaped straight towards him. He could hear the powerful motor roaring under full acceleration. The lights were almost on him now. He dodged to the right but the lights changed course with his every move. Almost instinctively, he faked a run to his left and then he dove to the right, hoping to land behind his car. He almost made it. The sedan hit him low, sending his pizza flying. Morrison was thrown onto the trunk of his own car and after accomplishing two and a half back flips, he slid off, hitting the pavement with a thud. Painfully lifting his head, all he could see were the taillights of the sedan disappear into the darkness. That was all he remembered.

"Hi, I'm Sharon, your nurse. Can I get you anything? A drink of water or perhaps a newspaper?"

The voice belonged to a perky young brunette with a movie actress face and figure to match. She bent over him, exposing just the right amount of cleavage.

"Are you the stewardess on this flight? Where are we going? Are we there yet?"

"We're not going anywhere, Mr. Morrison. You're in the hospital and I'm your nurse. You've had a nasty little accident."

"Oh. Yeah." He rubbed his head with his right hand. "I'm starting to get some fuzzy images. I kinda remember a bit. I was hit by a car, right? For a moment there I thought I must be in heaven" he said as he glanced at her ample bust. "Tell me, how badly am I busted up?"

"Well, sir, actually you're pretty lucky. Your left arm is broken and you've got a couple of badly bruised ribs, but other than that, you're fine. Now, can I get you anything?"

"Where's my pizza? I remember I had it just before I was hit."

"I'm sorry to report that your pizza was a total loss. Oh, while I think of it, now that you're awake, you have a couple of visitors. Shall I show them in? Campbell and South, think."

"Yes, by all means, show them in. I need to talk to them."

The detective admired her figure as she left the room. The door reopened minutes later and Bill and I walked in.

"Boy, you must really rate. Where do I sign up for a room in this joint? Every time I'm in the hospital, I get a room with six other guys and a nurse who looks like she plays for the Green Bay Packers on the weekend. How'd you end up with a foxy babe like that for a nurse?" asked Bill.

"I don't have a clue. I just woke up here. Maybe they save the good looking ones for cops. How did you two know I was in here, anyway?"

"We were having a cookout at Bills place. The steaks were hot, the beer was cold, and the radio was cranking out the oldies. All was right with the world. That is, until the ten o'clock news. Then we heard you'd been run down so we hustled right over. You made the big time news."

"I'm glad you guys came. I wanted to talk to you. This was no accident. Whoever it was, tried to run me down deliberately."

"Are you sure?" I asked. "It could have been a drunk who had one too many."

"No, it was deliberate. I tried to get out of the way but the guy followed me. The bastard aimed right at me all the way."

"Did you see what kind of car it was? Or anything?" asked Bill.

"It was a brown sedan; I think it was a Plymouth. The first part of the license number is 'BDD' but that's all I could get. Oh, and the plate was white."

"Hell, I'm surprised you got that much. If I would have been flung through the air by a speeding car, I'd be lucky to remember my name."

"I guess police training does come in handy once in a while. One thing they teach us at the academy is to immediately focus on the license plate, no matter how busted up or bleeding we might be. So I guess it was just instinct. Anyway, I'm going to have the boys down at the station run that partial through the computer and see if they can come up with a match. It's probably a long shot, but I sure would like to catch that SOB. He owes me a pizza."

Morrison used his good arm to push himself up a little straighter in the bed and then continued.

"You know, before this guy decided to use me for his own personal target, I did some serious thinking about what you guys told me from your conversation with the two Colonels. Apparently, our victims' reputation was above reproach. He appears to have been a bit naïve about certain things, but both men stated that he was a hell of a pilot. Both gentlemen noted that the wife was an artist. The one who was closest to the general stated that he never did trust her. Both mentioned that she had been investigated by the OSI."

"But that was standard procedure if a GI wanted to marry a local" I interjected.

"Ok, you're right on that point. We'll forget that part. The one colonel said he thought she was making fake paintings for sale abroad. Was she? In fact, was she ever involved in anything shady? We'll probably never know. Is she involved in anything illegal now? From meeting her, I'd say probably not. So where does that leave us?"

"We know someone tried to run you down. People generally go to those kinds of extremes for a good reason. I'd say that someone thinks you're getting too close to something. Maybe the counterfeit car guys" replied Bill.

"I thought about that. You might be right. If that's the case, you guys could be in grave danger, too."

"Ah, we'll be alright. We're both licensed to carry concealed handguns. Maybe we ought to go stakeout that old garage in Fayetteville. What do you think?"

"Sounds like a good idea to me" I said. "We might find out if that big guy I saw opening the gate for that Mercedes is the same one that killed the general."

"I think you two should stay away from there. If those guys are the ones who ran me down, they're playing for keeps. No, it's too dangerous. Besides, I don't have any evidence to get a search warrant anyway" replied Morrison.

"That's alright. We'll be careful."

"No, I mean it guys. Stay away from there. Let's work on the general's murder. I think I've got a few leads from those papers we picked up from his study. You two can help me check them out."

"Sure, Dave. Just as soon as they let you out we'll all start digging into them, ok?"

"All right. See you two later. I've gotta get some sleep."

"See you Dave."

With that, we both turned and left the room. As the door closed behind us, I turned to Bill.

"Ready to head for the garage tomorrow?"

"I thought he told us to stay away from there?"

"Come on, you know I have problems with authority figures. Besides, I took it more as a suggestion than anything else. Pick you up at seven?"

"Oh, what the hell. I can't let you go alone. You retired Air Force guys are pretty helpless at times."

Chapter 21

The next day I pulled into Bills driveway sharply at seven. Bill met me at the front door with a hot mug of coffee.

"Want to take my truck? I think it would probably blend in better in a junk yard."

"Well, you'd be right about it blending in, but if we need to get out of there in a hurry, I think the 'Vette is a better choice. We can hide it behind all the junk like we did last time."

"Ok, it's your baby. I'm game if you are. Let's go."

We climbed into the Corvette and I twisted the ignition key. The huge 427 rumbled into life. I backed out of the driveway and slipped the shifter into first. The rear tires squealed slightly as I let out the clutch a bit too quickly.

"Hey, be careful. You'll spill my coffee."

"Sorry, 'bout that. Did you remember the camera?"

"Sure did. Brought extra batteries and a doubler for the zoom lens. That'll bring the subject in twice as close. Got everything right here" Bill replied, patting the bag he had placed on the floor in front of him."

I retraced the roads we had taken just a week before. Once Wendals Garage came into sight, I drove slowly past it to make sure no vehicles were visible inside the rusty gate. As before, Bill got out and opened and closed the gate after I drove through. He returned to the car after closing it.

"This time when we hide the car, let's try to camouflage it a little, just in case" he said.

"Good idea. Why don't you look for something to use while I back down this row of junkers?"

Bill got out of the car and I put the Corvette in reverse. I turned my head around and slowly backed down between the wrecked automobiles.

"This might do the trick" said Bill, holding up an old piece of canvas.

"Yeah, and there's a piece of black plastic laying over there" I replied, closing the car door. "It'll probably help."

We stretched the canvas and plastic across the aisle between the junk cars, effectively hiding the Corvette.

"That should work fairly well unless someone really looks close" said Bill as he surveyed our handiwork.

"Now, let's climb up on top of that pile of old cars and set up the equipment. Oh, here's the camera bag."

I handed the bag to Bill and started climbing up the stack of junk cars piled precariously one on top of each other. Carefully I checked for a secure spot to place each foot and then felt for a solid handhold. Slowly but surely I ascended to the top. Once on the summit, I called down to Bill.

"Ok, come on up. Just be careful. Make sure you've got a good foothold. This stuff might not be too steady."

Bill scrambled up the junk pile quickly. At the top, he sat down the bag and carefully removed the camera and the accessories. After attaching the doubler and telephoto lens to the camera body, he reached back into the bag. This time he pulled out a short tripod. He mounted the camera onto it and attached a cable release.

"Now we're ready" he proclaimed. "All we have to do now is wait."

And wait we did. Early morning turned into afternoon. Two or three cars had driven down the lonely road but none of them had shown any interest in the deserted junk yard. Bill looked at his watch as the sun stood directly overhead.

"Want a sandwich, Gerr?"

"You brought lunch? What a lifesaver! I never gave it any thought. Too excited to get out here, I guess. Sure, I'll have one."

Bill delved into the camera bag and came out with a ham and cheese sandwich. He handed it over to me and then reached back in and came out with one for himself as well. As he unwrapped it, he reflected on the morning's lack of action.

"I'll bet cops really get bored on stakeouts. You know, we might sit here for weeks before anyone comes in here."

"Well, I'll agree it's not like you see on TV. And you're right, we may be wasting our time. I guess we'll just have to wait and see."

We finished lunch and settled back to relax as best we could. As the sun made its westward trek into late afternoon, a cloud of dust down the road announced the arrival of another car to the lonely road. A brown four door sedan slowly came into view. Bill swung the camera around and peered through the telephoto lens.

"Boy, this could be it" he exclaimed. "That's a brown Mercedes like you saw last time. Here, take a look."

I shifted my position so I could examine the newcomer through the camera. It looks like the same car, I thought. We'll know for sure if it turns in here."

Sure enough, as the car approached the junk yard it began to slow. Both of us could see the red glow of the cars brake lights in the dust cloud following it. The brown sedan pulled in front of the rusty gate and stopped. I pushed the shutter release on the camera. The front passenger door opened and the same burley man I'd seen on the previous visit got out. I zoomed the telephoto lens in as close as it would go and snapped another photo. The man opened the gate and the Mercedes drove through. He pulled it closed and walked to the garage while the driver turned the car around.

The driver pulled a set of keys from his pocket and tried several of them in the padlock that secured the door. He soon found the right one and the lock popped open. Both men disappeared into the run down garage.

Nothing happened for almost ten minutes. Then we heard a strange noise. Kind of a grating sound that appeared to be coming from the other end of the garage, the end that remained hidden from our vantage point.

"What the heck is that noise?" asked Bill.

"I'm not sure, it's familiar, though. Oh, hell. I know what it is! They're opening the rear door."

A split second later we heard a big block V8 engine cough into life inside the garage. We heard it rev a few times and then settle into a deep throated rumble.

"They're bringing out a car" I whispered to Bill. "I've gotta get a picture of this."

I aimed the camera at the far end of the garage and focused. A moment later a bright orange nose poked out of the door. The entire car rolled out and stopped. Leaving it idle, the burly man got out and closed the door. He walked back to the garage, apparently to pull down the overhead door. I snapped another picture.

"Well, there's my GTO Judge" said Bill. "Sure is pretty, isn't it?"

"Yeah, and if the quality is as good as the generals cars, somebody bought themselves a beauty. Even if it is a fake."

"Sh, here they come again."

The back door flung open and both men came out. Locking the door behind them, they each went to a car. The burly man went to the GTO; the other to the Mercedes. Both cars drove out the gate and stopped on the other side. This time, the sedan driver closed the gate. Once he was back behind the wheel, he motioned to the GTO. The orange car rocketed down the road with the Mercedes following in a more sedate manner.

"We've got some great shots. Let's head home and have a look at them."

When we got back to my house, I removed the data card from Bills digital camera. I popped it into a special holder and inserted that into the USB port on my computer. With a few clicks of the mouse, all the pictures we'd taken earlier in the day appeared.

"We've got some prize winning shots here, but I don't recognize either of these guys. We can probably have Morrison run the license plate, though. Here, Gerr, you have a look."

I turned the computer monitor over so I could get a better view of it. The first photo was of the Mercedes stopped at the gate. I had to admit, it was an excellent photo. Bill's right, I thought. That license plate ought to be a cinch to trace. When I glanced at the next photo, I almost shouted out loud!

"Bill," I exclaimed. "I know this guy! Look, the hefty one in the brown coat! That's the security guard at General Macomb's estate!"

Chapter 22

"You're right. It is the same guy. I'd recognize him anywhere. My favorite rent-a-cop.

I slid the rest of the photographs I printed off my computer across the desk towards Morrison.

"We've got a good clear license number on the Mercedes. How about running it through the computer?"

"Oh, I plan on it. By the way, I got a make on that car that ran me down. Just like I figured though, it didn't help. The car was stolen. We dusted it for prints but that was a dead end, too. May I keep these photos?"

"Sure. I've got them on my computers' hard drive so I can print as many as I want. You going to arrest the rent-a-cop?"

"Can't" replied the detective. He hasn't committed any crimes in my jurisdiction. At least not yet. I can investigate in those places, but I can't bust him for a crime he *might* have committed outside of my turf."

"Ok, you're the gumshoe. Listen, we'll catch you later. I promised the little woman I'd take her bowling tonight" said Bill.

"Yeah, see you later, Dave. My dance card's filled for the evening, too" I chimed in.

"Ok, take it easy, guys" answered the detective as he gave them a wave.

We left the police station and walked to Bills truck. The passenger door sagged on its hinges as I opened it to climb in. I pulled myself up onto the seat and lifted the door slightly to get it shut.

"You know, one of these days this door is going to fall right off. Probably with my hand attached."

"Ah, come on. This is one tough old truck. She's got another hundred thousand miles left in her. Beat out a few dents and give her a paint job, heck, she'd look good as new" replied Bill, patted the cracked and faded dashboard.

"Well, how about seeing if this rare classic will start so we can get down the road, ok?"

Bill twisted the key and the tired Chevy six cylinder coughed once and sputtered into a rough idle. He pulled the shift lever down into first gear and let out the clutch. The truck moved forward. Bill cranked the bus size steering wheel to the right and truck edged its way out of the parking lot.

"Hey, let's stop by Wal Mart before we head home. I'd like to pick up a couple of things."

"Sure, we can do that."

Bill turned at the town square and drove towards the store. Just as he pulled into the left turn lane to enter the stores' parking lot, a brown four door sedan whipped past. The driver signaled and drove onto the entrance ramp to US Route 15.

"Bill, look! There's the Mercedes! That's it! I know it is!" I exclaimed and pointed after it. "Quick, follow them!"

Bill quickly checked over his shoulder to make sure the right lane was clear and pulled out to follow the brown car.

"You realize I just ran a red light, right?"

"Yeah, yeah. If you get a ticket, we'll have Morrison fix it."

Bill followed the Mercedes down the entrance ramp and onto the highway. We were headed north and the sedan was slowly pulling away from us.

"Come on, Bill. Don't lose him!" I cried excitedly.

"Hey, give the poor old girl a break. I'll do my best, but I won't be able to sniff his tailpipe if he gets serious about it. He's probably got a two hundred horsepower advantage on me."

"And a hundred thousand miles less wear and tear. Just do the best you can. I'd really like to see where he's going."

The Mercedes kept going north and showed no signs that they were being followed.

"Where do you suppose they're going, Gerr? You know, this might be a wild goose chase. For all we know, they could be headed for New York or even farther. Heck, they might be going to Canada."

Just as I opened my mouth to reply, the sedans right hand turn signal began to flash amber. The car moved off the expressway and up the

Biglerville exit. Bill signaled and then followed at a discreet distance.

"Maybe they're stopping for gas" I suggested.

"Well, we'll find out shortly" replied Bill as he turned left, following the car directly into the small hamlet of Biglerville.

"I'd say you could get a little closer, Bill. They could turn off on some little back road and we might miss them. Besides, there's forty million beat up old pickup trucks in this neck of the woods; you could climb up their rear bumper and they'd probably never notice we're following them."

The sedan continued on for several miles. As it approached an intersection just outside of town, its amber turn signal began to flash again.

Bill shifted down into second gear and followed.

"These city boys are going to get lost running around back here if they're not careful" he said as he pulled the shift lever back down into high gear. "I get pretty confused on some of these roads myself."

The car turned right and drove a quarter of a mile then suddenly veered into an old, one lane dirt road and began to bounce towards a decrepit old pole barn about a hundred yards off the road.

"Better drive on past and hide the truck somewhere. We can sneak up on foot and see what they're up to" I said.

Bill nodded in acknowledgement and wheeled the truck in behind a small grove of pine trees. Both of us climbed out and gingerly closed the truck doors. We crept through the little woods to the tree line on the other side. Lying low to the ground, we surveyed the scene at the old barn. The two occupants of the car were just entering the building.

"Let's see if we can make it over there without getting caught. Don't forget to keep low" I said.

We both took off at a run, crouched low in an attempt to avoid being discovered. We made it across the open field without incident and flattened ourselves up against the back wall of the run down building.

"Ok, Gerr. We made it this far, what do we do now?" whispered Bill.

"Let's try to make our way around to that window. We might be able to hear something."

We quietly edged our way around the end of the building and down the side. Reaching the window, we huddled underneath it. It had been painted over years ago so looking through it was out of the question. The paint didn't stop voices from coming through, however. We could hear the men inside quite clearly.

"Hurry up. Get those new titles into the file. We've got other places to go" said the husky voice I identified as the security guard at the generals estate.

"Ok, ok. Hold your horses. I'm putting them in. Hey, by the way, what is a Sunbeam, anyhow? Don't they make mixers or appliances or something?" replied the other man. "This title is for a Sunbeam Tiger, ever hear of it?"

"I don't know. Some foreign junk, I guess. That's all the boss builds here. Come on, let's get going, ok? We've still got a shipment for the Shippensburg location to drop off."

"Alright, done. Lock the door and we're off."

The two men left the building and started the Mercedes engine. A second later it roared down the road leaving a cloud of dust in its wake.

"Quick, Bill. Back to the truck! We *have* to follow them now! They must have a whole chain of shops building counterfeit cars up and down the valley. We might be able to locate a few more of them if we can stick with that car."

We took off and made a mad dash for Bills truck. Bill hit the starter and grabbed the shifter at the same moment. The motor gave its customary cough and then it caught. The truck lurched backward onto the hard road. Its rearward progress came to an abrupt halt as Bill slammed on the brakes, yanked the shifter lever down into first gear, and let the clutch fly out, all in one motion. Smoke rolled off the rear tires as they searched in vain for traction. Finally the truck leaped forward and jolted down the road in chase.

"What kind of car were they talking about back there?" asked Bill. "I've never heard of a Sunbeam Tiger before."

"It's a little British sports car, something like an MG. Originally it was called the 'Alpine' and came with an anemic little four cylinder engine; it wasn't very fast but they were a lot of fun. In the mid 1960s, Carol Shelby started dropping high performance Cobra 289 V8s in them and calling them 'Tigers'. You've probably seen them and didn't even know it. Maxwell Smart on the old TV series 'Get Smart' drove one."

"Oh, yeah. Little red roadster, right? I do remember seeing it. You mean that thing had a V8 stuffed in it?"

"Sure did. Would be easy to fake, too. Just take an old Alpine body, drop in a 289, tack on a few Tiger emblems, and presto, you've doubled your money. I've got to hand it to this gang; they're smart. They've picked some of the easiest cars in the world to counterfeit and at the same time, make some of the highest profit margins in the business."

We finally made it back to the main road.

"Well, which way do you think they went? I'd say they probably went right because up the road a ways is a shortcut to Shippensburg and they did say they had a shipment for there."

"Assuming they know about the shortcut. Might as well give it a try."

Bill opened the old truck up as much as he dared in an attempt to make up lost ground between them and the Mercedes. At seventy five miles an hour, almost everything started to shake.

"Are you sure this thing will hold together at this speed?" I asked anxiously.

"Search me. I seldom drive it over sixty."

"Oh, great. We're cruising at warp speed in a bucket of bolts and you don't have a clue if it'll self destruct or not. I knew we should've brought the 'Vette."

"Hey, this is a Chevy. It'll hold together. If it was a Ford, we'd have something to worry about."

"Well, I guess that is one point in our favor. Just keep an eye open for that Mercedes. Hopefully they aren't playing Mario Andretti, too."

They must be, I thought to myself. Otherwise we'd have caught up with them by now. Unless they turned off the main road. I searched down every little side road and lane for any sign of the brown sedan. It was nowhere to be seen.

"They must have turned off somewhere by now" I muttered aloud.

"What'd you say, Gerr?" asked Bill as he wrestled with the steering wheel, trying his best to keep the truck in its lane.

"Oh, I was just thinking out loud. We should have caught up with them by now. They must have turned off somewhere. We might as well turn back and head for home."

"Alright. I'll turn around the next chance I get."

Bill started looking for a good place to turn around. The road made a sharp right turn around an old oak tree. As Bill manhandled the old Chevy around it, I grabbed his arm and pointed at the windshield.

"Look, I think that might be the Mercedes way up there! Doesn't that look like it to you?"

Bill squinted against the western sun. "Yeah, I think you might be right. We may as well stick it out. We're in a pretty good position to follow them now; close enough to see them, but far enough away that they won't notice us."

We fell silent for the next several miles. The road began to wind steeply uphill. Bill had to downshift into second gear to keep his momentum going. Still staying just out of sight, he coaxed the old truck up the steep, winding road.

"You want me to get out and help push?" I laughed.

"Ah, come on. This old girl got you this far, didn't she?"

"But will she get us back again, that's what I'm worried about."

Just as if it had been given a cue from some unseen movie director, the truck coughed twice and the motor died. Bill automatically reached for the ignition switch and gave it a twist. The starter whirred and turned the engine slowly but nothing happened.

"Oh, great. Now we're really stuck. Worse yet, those crooks are getting away."

"It's probably nothing serious. Come on, let's get the hood up and check it out."

Bill bounded out of the truck and had the hood up before I could even get my sagging door open. He was bent over the motor when I finally got there.

"See, I told you it was something simple" he said, pointing to a blue wire hanging by one strand from the ignition coil. "That wire came loose from the primary side of the coil. Probably from all that high speed driving we've been doing. Have you got your knife on you?"

I reached in my pocket and handed over my ever present Swiss Army knife. Bill pulled the one remaining strand of wire from the coil and, with the small knife blade, stripped off half an inch of blue plastic insulation. He then twisted the fresh wire strands together.

"Say, Gerr, there's a small crescent wrench in the glove box. Would you get it for me?"

I nodded and went back around to the passenger's side of the truck. Reaching through the window, I opened the glove compartment door and searched for the wrench. Just as I found it, I heard a vehicle coming down the road towards us. Shading my eyes from the sun, I peered through the trees for a glimpse of the oncoming car or truck. Suddenly I saw the unmistakable shape of a Mercedes Benz grill with its three pointed star perched proudly on top, rounding the curve a little over a tenth of a mile away. Quickly I ran around the front of the truck and buried my head under the hood next to Bill.

"Don't look up" I said tensely. "A Mercedes is coming down the road. It may not be the same one but let's not take any chances."

Bill did as I told him but as the car sped past, he tilted his head slightly to the left.

"That's the one all right. That's the same damn car we've been chasing all over the Cumberland Valley for the past hour. They weren't gone very long so their garage must be really close. Hand me that wrench and let's get this wire back on. Maybe we'll get lucky and find it."

Using the wrench, Bill unscrewed the nut from the primary post of the coil. He wrapped the new wire around the post and turned the nut back down snug with his fingers. After a final tightening, he tossed the wrench back to me and reached for the hood.

"There you go, my friend. All fixed. Let's go find their garage" he said as he slammed the rusty hood down tight. He twisted the key and the engine started immediately. Glancing in the mirror, he pulled out and started up the hill. When the truck reached twenty five miles an hour, he shifted into second.

"You know" Bill said, "that wire has probably been coming loose for quite some time. This old girls running better than she has in a long while."

"It does seem to be doing pretty good, doesn't it?" I replied.

We rode on in silence looking right and left. Suddenly I let out a yell and pointed off to the right.

"There! Look at that old barn! Let's try in there."

Bill nodded and turned the truck into a narrow, deeply rutted dirt lane. There was no gate to go through this time and we could drive right up to the building. Bill drove around to the far side, parking out of sight of the road. We got out and gingerly shut the truck doors.

The old barn must have been a masterpiece in its day. It wasn't large, but it had been rather ornate once upon a time. An intricate pattern was made into the bricks at the very top of each end to allow for ventilation. The end that could be seen from the road had a faded Mail Pouch tobacco advertisement painted on it. Several dozen of the split cedar shingles had fallen off the roof. This would be just the kind of run down building those guys would be looking for, I thought.

"Let's see if we can find some evidence that someone was here recently, like fresh tire tracks or something" I said to Bill.

Carefully we crept around to the front of the barn. After peeking around the corner to make sure no one was coming, we stepped in front of the huge barn door.

"Look, right here, Gerr. Tire tracks for sure. I've seen that pattern before but I can't place it."

"They look like Pirellis'. Not the cheap ones, either. If I had to take an educated guess, I would have to say they were probably on our missing Mercedes. Hey, what's this?"

I reached down and stuck my index finger into a black spot on the ground. Pulling it back, I rubbed the black substance between my index finger and thumb.

"Somebody was just here, all right. This is fresh oil. Let's check inside."

The front door was secured with a stout padlock. I tried the first window. It wouldn't budge, appearing to be barred from the inside. I tried the next one with the same results. The third window moved a bit, creaking as I pushed against it. Bracing myself, I gave one big push and suddenly the window flew open. Instead of the old musty farm smell I'd expected, the pungent odor of paint thinner hit me squarely in the face.

"This is the place, Bill. That smell is enough to knock you out. And I don't mean manure, either. They must have recently sprayed one in here. Let's check it out."

We eased ourselves through the smallish window. I reached into my pocket for my favorite flashlight. Flipping it on, I surveyed the inside of the old barn. It was set up in the same fashion as all the other garages we'd visited. Makeshift paint booth in the corner, workbench along the wall, file cabinets at the end of the workbench, and a spotlessly clean working area in the middle of the room.

"You know something" said Bill, "If I didn't know any better, I'd swear these guys were ex-military. You know, every place is set up exactly the same. It's like they have a regulation or something telling them how to set up their shops."

"By golly, I think you might be on to something there. Every place we've seen has been set up the exact same way. They could be former GIs."

"I wonder what they're building this time" Bill said, thinking half out loud.

"Well, let's check in the paint booth and find out" I replied.

Bill reached over and lifted the curtain on the end of the makeshift paint booth. Inside was a freshly painted blue Mercury Cougar."

"I'd say you're looking at a future Cougar Eliminator" I said. "I used to go to Vo-Tech school with a guy who had one of those. Same old story; change hoods, bolt on a spoiler, and tack on some decals and voila, instant Eliminator."

"They are making it look easy, aren't they? At least this time Morrison can check it out. This shop is on his turf."

"Hey, that's right! This is Adams County. Let's go tell him. He ought to be able to get a search warrant this time."

After carefully replacing the plastic curtain around the paint booth, we both checked to make sure everything was back where it had been. We went back to the window and retraced our steps to Bills truck.

Chapter 23

"Well, where in the hell are Lou and Butch? I thought they were supposed to be here at noon?"

"Patience, Randolph, patience. Lou gets relieved at noon and it will be a couple of minutes until he can make it here" replied the small oriental woman, speaking to the black butler.

Seemingly on cue, the doorbell began to chime. As it finished its pleasant melody, two burley men burst into the room.

"Hey, we made it. Now, what the hell are we doing here? I've only got an hour for lunch."

"Well, it's your fault, Lou. If you hadn't fucked up, we wouldn't be here in the first place" replied the butler coldly.

"What'd I do?"

"You ran down that cop in Gettysburg, you fucking idiot!"

"Sit down and shut up". Mrs. Malcomb rose to her feet. "Sit down and shut up, all of you. I'm still in charge here."

She walked around to the other side of the table and stood facing the men with both hands flat on the table.

"Look, we've got a good thing going here. I will not have any of you fools screwing it up. Lou, you moron, what the hell were you thinking?" she said in a voice that suddenly changed from demure oriental lady to cold, Bronx mob madam.

"Aw, I was only tryin' to scare him off" replied the big man squirming just a bit in his chair.

"Well, thanks to you, now that stupid cop is starting to look at our business interests as well as my husbands' unfortunate death" replied Mrs. Malcomb with an icy tone in her voice. "He's been asking a lot of insinuating questions lately. I don't know if he's found any of our shops yet but I've told our men to quickly finish the cars we've started and then close down."

"Does this mean we're finally going to get our money?" asked Butch.

"Look" replied Mrs. Malcomb coldly. "You know the deal. The money is in the Caymans. You know what it's for, and you know we'll all benefit beyond any of your wildest dreams when this is over. Now, that is the last time we are going to mention the money. We have the project to deal with and it must be our number one priority. Nothing else matters. End of discussion."

"Yes, madam. Sorry" all the men muttered in unison, their eyes all staring at the floor.

"Good, now get the hell out of here and get back to work. I have things to do."

After they left, she quickly walked out of the parlor and up the stairs to the library. She entered and pulled the heavy walnut pocket doors closed behind her. Locking them securely, she turned to survey the room. There were more than three thousand books on six rows of shelves completely surrounding the four walls. She went directly to the back wall and searched through the books on the third shelf. Sitting between a second edition of *Tom Sawyer* and a signed copy of *Huckleberry Finn* sat a rather ragged copy of an old world atlas.

She reached up and took hold of it by the top of the spine. She tilted it forward towards her and was greeted by a low whirring sound from somewhere behind the bookshelves. Almost silently, the center section of shelves swung outward into the library. Mrs. Malcomb slipped behind the shelf and into a small room. She reached for a switch, twisted it, and suddenly light flooded the room.

The room, if you could call it that, was only about five feet by ten feet. It would probably be better described as an alcove. The only furniture in the room was a small table and chair. A naked light bulb, one of the old fashioned Thomas Edison style, hung on a single wire from the ceiling. On the table sat a powerful short wave radio.

Mrs. Malcomb grabbed the door and pulled it closed behind her. She turned her attention to the radio. Flipping on the power switch, she seated herself on the chair and began to tune the receiver. Suddenly a voice crackled from the speaker.

"This is Papa Bear calling Mama Bear. Come in Mama Bear. Over."

"This is Mama Bear" answered Mr. Malcomb. "Code word for today is 'golden'. Over."

"Code authenticated. How do you read? Over."

"I have you five by five. And me? Over."

"Five by five as well. What is the status of the project? Over" came the same voice.

"Project temporarily on hold. A local cop is nosing around. He's been getting a bit too close lately. I've had to shut things down for a few months. Over."

"Disapproved. There can be no delay. The project will continue. You will not let the cop stop us. Over."

"This cop will be much more careful now. It's a risk I don't think we can afford to take at this time. Over."

"He will not be allowed to hold things up. The final phase of this project will start on schedule. That is the final word on the subject. Over and out."

With that outburst, the radio fell silent.

"Bastard" she muttered under her breath as she switched off the radio. She turned the door handle and opened the bookshelf door. Reaching back, she twisted the light switch off as she left the room.

Chapter 24

Clang. The shovel stuck a rock as the man attempted to plunge it into the earth.

"Don't worry, folks" he laughed. "A little rock isn't going to slow the finest affordable housing development in south central Pennsylvania. Royal Realty will be retiring this ceremonial golden shovel and breaking ground with the real equipment beginning very shortly. We expect the first group of houses to be ready to move into by early next summer. We then plan to finish a new section every six to eight months after that. Ladies and gentlemen, we pledge to you that ninety percent of the labor force building these homes will be hired right here locally. We intend to keep your local tax dollars right here in your community. And now, Mr. Mayor, I'd like to hand the floor back to you."

"Thank you, Mr. Revson. I'm proud to have you and your company here in our community today. We look forward to working with you as we build a better future for our citizens. Again, thank you, sir."

The mayor reached out his hand and the other man took it and shook it vigorously. Side by side, they both walked off towards the hoard of television and radio media that awaited them.

Chapter 25

I opened the newspaper and reached for my coffee to take a sip. I quickly scanned the front page for anything interesting. Nothing in particular caught my fancy, so I turned the page and continued looking for interesting news. I flipped one page and then another.

I was just ready to turn the page again when something stopped me. Something on the previous page suddenly registered with my brain. I turned the page back. There, on page 5 was a photo and a story announcing a new housing development.

"Well, I'll be damned" I exclaimed out loud. "Look at who's in that picture!"

I carefully examined the photo and then read the story associated with it over and over. Gotta call Dave on this one. I reached over and grabbed the cordless phone. Pushing the buttons I waited to hear the phone ring on the other end of the line.

"Detective Morrison, may I help you?"

"Dave, Gerry. Have you looked at the *Times* today?"

"Well, I glanced at it; I didn't actually read it. Why?"

"Check out page 5. Especially the photo."

"All right, give me a minute" Morrison replied.

I could hear the detective open the newspaper. I heard the pages rustle as Morrison leafed through them.

"Ok. I've got the article you're talking about. What about it?"

"Look closely at the photo. Don't you recognize the guy with the shovel?"

Morrison readjusted the paper so he could get a better look at it. "Hey, you know, that looks a lot like that black butler of Mrs. Macomb's."

"It *IS* Randolph! Only thing is, he's listed in the article as a Lawrence Revson, CEO of Royal Realty. How do you suppose he went from butler to real estate tycoon so quickly?" I asked.

"I don't know but I think we should find out. Oh, by the way, we executed the search warrant yesterday on the barn you guys found. We grabbed a lot of evidence, but really, it's still pretty generic stuff. Unless we can find some good prints or something really compelling, we don't have much to go on. These guys covered their tracks pretty well, from what I've been able to see so far."

"I kinda figured that; we're not dealing with idiots" I replied. "Do you think you can find anything out about Royal Realty?"

"I'll find out everything there is to know about that bunch, you can bet on that" answered the detective firmly. "I'll call you when I get something."

"Ok, thanks. Talk to you later."

I hung up the phone and then pushed the 'talk' button again. I dialed Bills number and waited."

"Yeah?"

"That's a hell of a way to answer the phone" I said.

"Sorry. You woke me out of a sound sleep. I was takin' a nap."

"Well, listen. I just hung up with Morrison. Remember I told you about General Morrison's butler, Randolph?"

"Yeah, I remember. What about him?"

"Well now all of a sudden he's the CEO of a real estate company. Apparently they're going to build a housing development out in East Berlin."

"I'm sorry. I thought you just said he was going to build houses. What the hell does a butler know about building houses?" exclaimed Bill.

"That's what we'd all like to know" I replied.

Chapter 26

The next day I was just replacing the last spark plug in the Corvette and cleaning and setting the gap on each one when the phone rang. I put down the ratchet and socket, walked across the garage, and picked up the cordless extension.

"Hello."

"Gerry, this is Dave. You busy?"

"I just got done tuning the "Vette, why?"

"I've got some info you really ought to see. How about meeting me at the office? 'Bout an hour? Oh, and bring Bill. Ok?"

"Well, I'll be there. I'll have to call Bill and see if he can make it."

"Alright" replied Morrison. See you shortly."

I hung up the phone and dialed Bills number. Bill answered and I told him the news. We agreed to meet at my place and drive to the office from there.

We arrived at the station and made our way to Morrison's office.

"Hi guys. Glad you came. Let's get right to it."

He opened a large manila folder lying on his desk and spun it around for us to see.

"This is what I found on Royal Realty. It's a shell corporation owned by another shell corporation."

"So who's it supposedly owned by?" asked Bill.

"Our old friends, Classic Investments."

"Are you serious? Those guys that are faking the collectible cars? What do they know about houses?" said Bill.

"I wouldn't have a clue, but that's who owns Royal Realty. Of course the address turns out to be a vacant lot. No big surprise there. That's just standard operating procedure."

"So," I asked "do we know who runs Royal Realty?"

"The name on the company papers is Lawrence Revson but of course we know he's Randolph the butler. I don't know if anyone else is in on it."

"Ok" said Bill. "We do know now that Classic Investments and this Royal Realty are connected. It seems to me that maybe Randolph and Mrs. Malcomb are more than simply employee and employer. It sure looks like they're more partners than anything else. I wonder how they got together in the first place."

"You know, that's an excellent observation" said Dave. "That's also a great question, how did they get together? And I might add, who else in involved? Gerry, do you suppose Randolph could have met Mrs. Malcomb in the military?"

"Well, sure. Of course that's possible. And I know just how we can find that out! Bill, do you remember Chief Lucas?"

"Yeah. He'd probably be happy to help out. You have his number?"

"Sure do. Dave, do you mind if we use the phone? We need to call the Air Force World Wide

Locator. They can tell us if those two were ever stationed together."

"Sounds like a plan to me. Go for it."

By now you know that there are several items that I always have with me. One of those items is a flashlight. Another is a Swiss Army knife. And one more is a notebook and pen. I pulled out my ever present notebook and flipped through the pages. Finally I found the number, picked up the receiver and dialed the Chief's number. After a couple of rings, the phone was picked up on the other end.

"Locator, Chief Lucas. May I help you?"

"Chief, Sergeant Campbell. How are you doing?"

"Good, Sarge. How's the investigation going? Any news?"

"Actually we aren't making too much progress. But we're hoping you can change that by helping us again. Do you know any way we can find out if certain individuals were ever stationed at the same location at the same time? I'm putting this call on speaker so Bill and Detective Morrison can hear, also."

"Sure, no problem. Just give me the names and I'll let this big old computer sort things out."

"Ok. First, Mrs. Malcomb. Next, a Randolph Severs. And if you can find anyone else either one of them may have been close to. Think you can come up with anything?"

"We'll know in a few seconds, Sarge. Let me enter the info."

We could all hear the Chief furiously tapping on a keyboard in the background. Then we heard a printer kick into gear.

"I think I might just have what you're looking for, sarge" came the Chiefs voice over the speaker phone. "When our squadron left 'Nam, they went to Germany. That's when I cross trained so I came back to the states. Mrs. Malcomb and the general were sent to Ramstein Air Base. Senior Airman Randolph Severs was also assigned to the same unit at Ramstein. He was convicted of stealing from a local merchant and given a bad conduct discharge in 1972. However, he wasn't alone. He was caught with two army personnel. One, a sergeant named Louis Burgmeister and a private named Frederick White, nicknamed

'Butch'. Both of these guys also got bad conduct discharges. Does that help, guys?"

"You bet it does! It would help even more if we had pictures of all these guys" I said.

"No problem, if you have a fax handy."

"Sure, Chief" replied Morrison. "Here's the number."

The detective recited the fax number for the Chief. Within minutes the fax machine clattered into action and spit out several sheets of paper. Each one contained the mug shot of a former military member.

"Well, now I know there is something rotten around here" said Morrison. "I knew damn well I didn't like that bastard!"

"I should have known, too" I replied. "That Lou guy is the security guard at the Macomb's housing community. And that other guy was with Lou at Wendals Garage when they dropped off those fake titles and VIN tags."

"So, is this info going to help you catch the general's killer, guys?" asked Chief Lucas over the phone.

"Absolutely, Chief. We really owe you for this one. Thanks so much."

"Just catch him, sarge. Just catch him."

"We will, Chief. And when we do, you'll be the first to know. I promise you that. Thanks again."

With that, I pushed the 'Off' button on the speaker phone.

"Well, fellows, now we know all these guys are connected and both companies are connected. And we know how they are connected. We just don't know what they're up to. It seems to me that since they all met in Germany, that would be the place to pick up the next clue."

"You certainly don't figure on Adams County financing a trip to Germany for any of us, do you?" asked Morrison.

"Well, no. I didn't figure the taxpayers would spring for anything quite so extravagant. But I do have an Idea" I replied.

"Go ahead, Gerr. Clue us in" said Bill.

"Ok. Remember, I'm retired Air Force. One of those almost forgotten benefits we have is the right to fly free on military aircraft if a space is available. What that means is, if there are empty seats on a flight to Europe, I can ride along and it won't cost the good taxpayers of Adams County a cent."

"And of course you can take along a close friend" said Bill.

"Ah, that would be a no" I replied. "Sorry. No can do. It's for retirees and their spouses only. I figure I can probably get a flight out of Andrews next week; they usually have lots of flights heading to and from Europe. I'll stay a week or two, maybe visit the Porsche factory and write a story about it."

"Sounds like a good idea to me" said Morrison.

Chapter 27

I spent the next several days making plans for my trip. I checked on flights and reserved lodging at Ramstein Air Base for a week. I arranged to meet with officials at the American Embassy in Berlin. Morrison provided me with papers making me an official deputy through his office. This would allow me to conduct an official investigation on the Malcomb murder and review any official papers that I might find necessary.

The flight over was uneventful, landing at Lajes Field in the Azores to refuel and then on to Ramstein. I deplaned, went through customs and checked into my quarters. The following day I rented a car and took a quick drive up the autobahn to Berlin for a visit to the American Embassy. The next day I drove across the base to visit with the security police.

"Good morning, sir. May I help you?" asked the Staff Sergeant manning the information desk.

"You may. I'm retired Master Sergeant Gerry Campbell. I have an appointment with

Captain Small." I pulled out my passport and my retired military identification card and pushed them across the desk to the sergeant.

The desk sergeant checked my identification against his appointment book. Satisfied that I did, indeed, have an appointment with his boss, he lifted the phone and called the squadron commander.

"Captain, Sergeant Campbell is here. Should I send him down?"

"Go ahead."

The sergeant turned back to me as he put down the receiver. "The captain said to send you down to his office. Just follow that hallway; it's the second door on the left." He pointed to a hall on the right side of his desk.

"Thanks, sarge."

I headed down the hall, found the correct office and knocked.

"Come in, Sergeant."

I entered and sat facing the captain.

"Sergeant, Let me be the first to say I'm glad you're working on General Malcomb's murder. The entire Air Force has been devastated by this tragedy. I have to say, however, I was shocked to find that the trail led across the pond to us here. You believe that these ex GIs were involved?"

"Yes, sir. We have received evidence that the individuals I emailed you about were, in fact, involved. Have you found anyone who knew them when they were stationed here?"

"I did. I had my investigators look up the people they hung out with, their former neighbors, and even a few that retired and stayed on over here. My folks interviewed them and I've got the transcripts right here for you. I figured that would save you a lot of time and trouble. If you want to talk with any of the people listed in the transcripts, their phone numbers are included. Is there anything else we can do for you, sarge?"

"I don't know, sir. Let me take all this info back to my quarters and read through it. I'll let you know tomorrow. Thanks very much."

I left the captain and returned to my quarters. I studied the transcripts very closely.

There was one person who intrigued me and I wanted to talk to him personally. The paperwork said he didn't have a phone, but he hung out in a local beer garden.

Later that night I went to the pub and met with the old gentleman. I bought him beer and he told me of his time with Randolph, Butch and Lou. I couldn't wait to get back and tell the guys this story.

I didn't go straight back, however. Like I planned, I took a side trip to Stuttgart to visit the Porsche plant. Being a registered journalist, I was given the VIP tour which included the museum. I went through two sets of batteries in my digital camera, shooting photos of some of the most priceless artifacts in automotive history. This was a once in a lifetime opportunity and I made the absolute best of it.

Chapter 28

When I returned to the states, we decided to all meet at my house.

The doorbell chimed invitingly.

"Come on in" I called out.

The door opened and Bill walked in, closely followed by Detective Morrison.

"This is the first time you've been here, isn't it, Dave? Beer's over there in the 'fridge". I pointed towards the kitchen. Morrison opened the side by side refrigerator and selected a Sam Adams. "You want one, Bill?"

"Yeah, I'll have a Lite, whatever Gerr's got."

Morrison grabbed a Miller Lite for Bill.

"Pick a seat and we'll get started" I said, gesturing towards the easy chairs surrounding the huge fireplace in the center of the living room.

"Well, Gerr, let's have all the juicy details" said Bill. "What did you find out?"

"Guys, prepare yourselves for a hell of a story. The first thing I did was visit the embassy. I got all the info they had on our friends. Then I talked with the Security Police and the Provost Marshall. The chief of the Security Police had his investigators talk with anybody still alive who was around when those guys were there. He gave me transcripts of all their interviews. Most were dead ends, but there was one old guy that intrigued me so I went to talk with him myself. He told me a story that you just will not believe."

"His name is Dieter Christoph. He's an 88 year old former Nazi sailor. He was on board a U boat at the end of the war. U-677. Have either of you ever heard of the Odessa?"

"Yeah. I saw the movie" replied Bill.

"What movie?"

"The Odessa File. You know, that movie that chick with all the tattoos dad is in" Bill replied.

"That made absolutely no sense at all" I said. "What the hell are you talking about?"

"Oh, you know who I mean. Angelina somebody."

"Angelina Jolie, per chance?"

"Yeah, that's the one. Her dad was in it."

"Oh, yes. Jon Voight. Now I know who you're talking about."

"I'm afraid you'll have to fill me in" Morrison chimed in.

"Well, at the end of World War II there were a lot of Nazis who wanted to keep Hitler's dreams alive. They wanted to build a Fourth Reich. To do this, they formed a secret organization known as the Odessa to further that goal. First, however, they had to protect current Nazis from capture and they had to save the valuables they had plundered from all over Europe. Without money to finance this organization, the whole thing would have fallen through right then and there."

I stopped for a moment to take a swig of beer.

"Dieters submarine left Germany just as the war was ending. It had a skeleton crew and was loaded down with stolen gold. The plan was to sail to Argentina where most of the high ranking Nazis had already gone. There, the gold would finance their life while they planned their return."

"But they never made it. The original route was planned to cross the Atlantic towards the U.S. coast and then turn south. They figured this late in the war, all the destroyers that were out looking for U boats would be closer the European coast and nowhere near America. But when they attempted to make the turn towards South America, the rudder malfunctioned. They couldn't steer the thing. It was night so they surfaced to shoot the starts and find out exactly where they were at."

"So, Gerry, did they call for help then?" asked Morrison.

"Dave," Gerry replied. "There was no one out there. These guys were totally on their own. If they got caught they would have been shot or sent to prison. They couldn't contact anyone."

"Anyway, when they surfaced, they found out the tide was taking them towards the mouth of the Chesapeake Bay and there wasn't anything they could do about it. The captain called the crew together for a meeting. He gave them their options. If their drift continued, they would run aground on the Virginia shore. If that happened, their mission would be discovered and the gold would be confiscated. With their skeleton crew, there really wasn't any chance they could fix the rudder. Their only chance was to scuttle the sub in the relatively deep water just off the shore."

"So, then what happened? How'd they get back to Germany?"

"Well, hang on a minute, let me grab another beer" I replied.

I went to the fridge and came back with another cold bottle. "Ok, now remember, these guys were Odessa, fanatical Nazis. They had orders not to let the gold fall into anybody else's hands. They also wanted it somewhere it could easily be gotten to, if need be. And the bottom of the sea was simply out of the question."

"So the first order of business was to sink the sub. They finally got the sub on the bottom in about thirty five feet of water, about a hundred and fifty yards offshore. They swam to the beach and hid in the woods. Now, remember, this was 1945. This country wasn't nearly as built up as it is nowadays. All that area down there was just country back then. So here they were, stuck in a foreign country and none of them spoke English. It turned out, however, that the mechanics mate had visited America as a teenager back in the 1930s. His family had relatives on the east coast in the one area of the country that still spoke German on a pretty regular basis. Anybody want to take a wild guess where that might be, fellows?"

"The only place I could think of is our very own Pennsylvania Dutch country. Heck, back then lots of folks spoke German and it was a lot more rural than it is now" exclaimed Bill.

"And you would be correct, Grasshopper" I replied.

"So what happened next?" asked Morrison.

"Well, they made themselves a plan. There was diving equipment on the sub. So they stole a couple of trucks and with the diving equipment, salvaged the gold off of the sub. They loaded the trucks and drove north. Traveling at night, they made their way slowly to Pennsylvania, following only the back roads. Dieter said it seemed like it took forever."

I paused for another sip of beer. "Finally they made it to East Berlin. They found the mechanics mates relatives, who hid them in their barn. Then they had to find a place to hide the gold."

"So, where is it?" asked Bill eagerly.

"Well, they didn't have time to look around much. They couldn't go running around in the daytime; it was way too risky. Suddenly, however, they had a stroke of good luck. Some old guy in town died. The local cemetery dug his grave on a Friday and covered it until the funeral on Monday. That left the grave open all weekend. So, under the cover of darkness, they took the gold to the cemetery. They dug the grave several feet deeper and put the gold in. After covering it lightly with dirt, they had it made. The funeral home put the guys casket on top of it and it's been there ever since."

"That *is* an incredible story" exclaimed Morrison. "But, what does it have to do with our friends at Classic Investments?"

"They are the only people that Dieter ever told the story to. They were all hanging out together at a beer garden one day. They started talking with Dieter and he let it slip that he was a former Nazi sailor. Fascinated, they started buying him beers. They got him pretty drunk and he ended telling them that story."

"Kind of like 'Old Johnny', remember Gerr?" said Bill.

"Who's 'Old Johnny'?" asked Morrison.

"Old Johnny is a guy we used to know. We were in a bar in Waynesboro one day having a few cold ones and 'Old Johnny' got himself pretty drunk. Well, you see, 'Old Johnny' used to work for Al Capone in Chicago back in the twenties. When he got really drunk that day, he told us all about the St. Valentine's Day Massacre. He never said anything about it when he was sober; it only happened that one time. It's funny, Bill, I thought about 'Old Johnny' when Dieter told me this story."

"So, you think this is for real?" asked Morrison.

"Why would he lie?" I replied. "Hell, he's old. He's not going to live much longer. I totally believe him."

"Ok, let's say we all believe him" said Bill. "I still don't understand what that has to do with Classic Investments and Royal Realty."

I shifted in my chair and reached for my beer. "I think I've got it figured out. They planned to get the gold a day or two after Dieter told them about it. But they had to get back to the states first. Then they needed money. This was going to be a vastly expensive undertaking."

"Right", replied Morrison. "And they couldn't just walk into East Berlin and start digging holes all over the place. Especially in a cemetery. So they had to figure out how to legally get near the land the gold is on and then they could simply dig it up at their leisure. Do I have it correct so far?"

"That's the way I have it figured. So then they needed a supply of cash to purchase the land. I figure that's why they came up with the fake collector car scam. They used the profits to buy the land that Royal Realty say they're going to build the housing development on. Only thing is, there won't be any housing development. They'll bring in some heavy equipment, start moving some dirt around, dig up the gold, and be in some far off foreign country before anyone knows what the hell hit 'em."

"Damn, this is one twisted story. So, really all we have to do is go watch the grave where the gold is buried and then pick them up, right?" asked Bill.

"Well, unfortunately there's one small problem. Dieter can't remember the name on the grave they used for the gold."

"That still shouldn't be too big a problem" said Morrison. "We can just surround the whole cemetery and watch where they go."

"Ok" I said. "I got a friend who's a State Constable over that way. I'll ask him to keep an eye on the place and phone me when Royal Realty brings in the equipment and breaks ground."

"That's a pretty good idea. I know a judge who'll give me a warrant anytime I need one, so when he calls you, you call me and I'll call my judge."

Chapter 29

A fortnight went by. I wrote an article on my trip to the Porsche factory and a couple of others in that time. Bill went on a weeklong fishing trip to Lake Erie. Late Friday night my phone rang.

I grabbed the cordless extension and pushed the 'talk' button. "Hello".

"Gerr, this is Andy, over in East Berlin."

"Hey, Andy. How goes it?"

"Good. Listen, I called because the Royal Realty folks just moved in some heavy equipment. They brought in a D9 Cat and a backhoe, along with a few other assorted bits and pieces. They started bringing the stuff in late this afternoon. I figure they'll start early Monday."

"Yeah, sounds like it to me. Thanks a lot, Andy. I owe you lunch."

Chapter 30

"Got the warrant?"

"Check" replied Morrison.

"Got the binoculars?"

"Check" said Bill.

"Is everyone armed?"

"Damn right!" we all exclaimed in unison.

"Good. How about your earwigs? Let's check them."

"Got you loud and clear" said Bill.

"You're coming in five by five here" I replied.

"Ok" said Morrison. "Everyone raise their right hand. Now, will you obey the laws of the Commonwealth of Pennsylvania, obey the orders of those appointed over you, and support and defend the Constitution of the United States, so help you God?"

"We will" Bill and I both replied.

"Good, then by the powers granted me by the Commonwealth of Pennsylvania and the County of Adams, I hereby declare that you are both official deputies." He reached into his jacket pocket and pulled out two silver badges. "Here you go, fellows. Pin them on, you're now legal lawmen!"

"Cool, kind of looks like it belongs there, doesn't it?" said Bill as he admired the badge now proudly displayed over his left breast pocket.

"Great. Now let's move in, shall we?" said Morrison. "Each of you take a corner of the cemetery to stake out and watch for any movement. Once we see them start any piece of equipment, we'll slowly move in. Watch to see which grave they head to and then we'll grab them."

"Sounds like a plan. Let's do it."

It was four thirty Monday morning. The cemetery was as quiet as, well, a cemetery. There were only a couple of lights on in the small hamlet of East Berlin. Each of us slowly made our way to a corner of the graveyard. I had the northeast corner. I found a rock behind a large holly bush to sit on. This looks like a perfect spot, I thought to myself. Now all I have to do is sit back and see what happens.

Time passed slowly. The sun slowly peaked over the hills to the east. There ought to be some action soon, I thought. My thoughts were abruptly interrupted by the earwig crackling in my ear.

"See anything yet?" asked Morrison"

"Not so far" I replied. "How about you, Bill?"

"Absolutely no movement over here" said Bill. "Don't you think someone would be here by now?"

"Yeah, it is after seven. I'm beginning to wonder if they're going to show today or not" answered the detective.

"You think maybe we should move in for a closer look?"

"Gerr, I think we should. But listen, take it very slow, guys. They just may be running late and if they are, we don't want to spook them off."

Each of us came out of his hiding place and slowly walked his way toward the middle of the cemetery. We took a couple of steps, looked in all directions, and then took a few more. Occasionally we would hunker down behind a headstone for cover. I slowly made it over to the D9 Caterpillar and took refuge behind it. Again the device in my ear came alive.

"Guys, we've got a problem" said Morrison. "You two better come see this."

"Where are you?" asked Bill. "It's still a little dark over in this corner."

"No problem. I'll shine my flashlight. Just follow it over here."

Morrison switched on his pocket flashlight and pointed it to the west. Both of us saw the beam and followed it to the source. When we arrived, we were shocked at what lay before us. Morrison stood beside an open grave with its coffin carelessly thrown aside.

"The bastards beat us to it" He slammed his fist into his hand in frustration. "They beat us. They must have been out here and dug it up on Saturday. Damn, that gives them over a day head start."

"So what do we do now" asked Bill.

"One thing we need to do is write down the VIN numbers of all this equipment so we can run them and find out who they're actually registered to. Then we need to get back to the Bat Cave and get some APBs out."

"Bat Cave? APB's?"

"Headquarters, Bill." I said. "All Points Bulletins."

"Oh, yeah. I knew that."

Chapter 31

Morrison's office was a blur of activity. I was furiously pounding away at the computer keyboard. Morrison was calling other police departments. Bill was checking various records and comparing them with the reports I was generating from the computer.

"Ok, guys, what have we found?"

"Well," I said. "We've discovered that Royal Realty does, in fact, own all of that equipment, lock stock and barrel. Apparently they figured that buying the stuff wouldn't raise as many red flags as renting. We also found that they recently bought two Ford box trucks. Again, I guess they figured renting might cause lots of questions and stealing them would really be a dumb move. Hell, they've got plenty of cash; might as well buy them."

"We figure they bought the trucks to transport the gold in. Only question is, are they going to fly it out of the country or are they going to put it on a boat?" said Bill.

"Anybody have an idea how much gold we're talking about here?" asked Morrison.

"About three tons is what Dieter estimated. Now, since they measure gold in troy ounces, that means about 72,000 ounces. In 1945 gold was worth $37 an ounce. That would make the subs cargo worth about 2.6 million dollars." I replied.

"Right, but that was World War II value. How much is it worth today?"

"About a hundred and thirty million."

"Whew. Now I understand why they could afford to spend so lavishly to find this haul. Heck, I figured they spend around two million on just the land and the equipment. Damn, that was a small price to lay out for one hell of a payday!"

Morrison continued. "So, if they've got three tons of gold, they obviously can't just put that on a commercial airliner because that would bring the Feds into this. And that's too much weight for a small, private plane. So they must be going to take it out by boat."

"Makes sense" said Bill. "They'd need someone with a pilot's license for a plane anyway, but anybody can run a boat."

"Yeah, that's true" I said. "But that's still a hell of a lot of weight for a boat. Unless it's a damn big boat."

"Right. You'd almost think they'd need a yacht to carry that much gold. You don't suppose they went out and bought a yacht, do you?" asked Bill.

"It's very possible, Gerr. Why don't you heat up that keyboard and see if you can find any registration records for any new acquisitions for Royal Realty. Oh, and try under Classic Investments, too" said Morrison.

"Good Idea. I'll get right on it."

While I worked the computer, Bill and the detective poured over maps of the local area. They knew the closest navigable water was the Susquehanna River. If the gang had gone there, they could have loaded the gold on a shallow draft boat and made their way down river to the Chesapeake Bay. That seemed like the most logical answer.

"Well, guys. There are no boats registered to either Royal Realty or Classic Investments. Not in Pennsylvania, Maryland, Delaware, or New

Jersey. I did, however, find a yacht rented by Royal Realty from a yacht rental agency in Aberdeen, Maryland" I said. "Looks like one of them went down there and brought the boat up river. Only question is, where are they going to meet to load the gold?"

"Listen, guys. I've done a good bit of fishing on the Susquehanna. I happen to know there's a pretty good marina just on the other side of the Maryland line. There's no way they could get any closer because there are a couple of dams in the way" replied Bill. "I'd almost bet that would be where they plan to load up. Besides it's a straight shot right down Route 30, which would make it quicker, too."

"You two just might make pretty fair detectives yet" laughed Morrison. "Check your weapons and ammo. Everybody head for my car."

With the red light flashing, Morrison flew down the Lincoln Highway as fast as he dared, using the siren sparingly. He only used it when he needed to get a slower moving vehicle out of the way. We passed through New Oxford in no time flat. Morrison made Abbottstown minutes later. He furiously sawed back and forth with the steering wheel trying to keep the heavy four door sedan under control as he virtually slid around the traffic circle in the center of town. The rear wheels clawed the asphalt in an attempt to grab some traction. They finally found some and the car rocketed down Route 30.

"Whoa there, Mario Andretti! Let's get there alive, shall we?" I yelled over the wail of the siren.

"Don't whine" Morrison yelled back. "You're wearing a seat belt and we've got airbags!"

I'm in the car with a mad man, I muttered to myself.

The car ate up the miles. Very soon we were passing the York Airport, just on the outskirts of York city.

"Hey, look at that!" exclaimed Bill as he pointed to the right. "There's an old DC-3 on the runway. Haven't seen one of those in years."

"Yeah, and look at that guy waving at them. It looks like he's trying to get their attention. Dave, does your radio get FAA frequencies? I'd like to know if they're trying to get the plane on the radio" I asked.

"I think so" replied Morrison. "Try one of those buttons. I've got to watch the road."

I reached down to the police radio and began pushing the different buttons.

"3794 come in. Please acknowledge. 3794 you have not filed a flight plan. Please acknowledge" the radio crackled.

"Sounds like they're having a bit of trouble over there" said Bill. "I thought all United States registered tail numbers started with 'N'.

"Well they do. But when it's a US tail number plane inside the US, the air traffic controllers generally just drop the 'N' when they hail the plane" I replied.

"3794 come in. You are not cleared for takeoff. I repeat, you are not cleared for takeoff. You have not filed a flight plan. Shut down your engines immediately."

"Do you find this just a little interesting? Don't you think we ought to investigate that plane?" I asked.

"Look, we've got to get to that marina! We don't have time to screw around. Sounds like an FAA problem to me" answered Morrison.

"It is. But I've never seen a real DC-3. That baby is over sixty years old; it's a real antique! I sure would like to get an up close look at it. Look at it this way, Dave, even if their boat leaves the marina, it'll still be on the river heading down to the Chesapeake. It's not like we're going to lose them."

"I'd rather catch them before they leave. I really don't want to try and follow them all over the east coast" said Morrison.

Bang! Just then a shot rang out.

"Hey, that came from the airport!" yelled Bill.

"Looks like we're going to investigate after all. Hang on!"

Morrison cranked the wheel hard to the left and slammed his right foot to the floor. The big sedan spun 180 degrees, smoke erupting from its rear tires as they spun wildly on the roadway. The car bolted towards the airport leaving a foul smelling cloud of tire smoke in its wake.

Morrison bounced across the tarmac to the control tower. Sliding to a stop, he threw the door open and ran in a crouch to the door.

"You two stay put until I call for you. Ok?" he yelled back to us.

"Ten four, Dave."

The detective reached the door, threw it open, and flung himself inside.

"We heard a shot" he exclaimed as he flashed his badge. "What's going on here?"

"I'm Reggie Sherman, the head controller. That DC-3 is trying to take off without a flight plan. The FAA requires a flight plan for any plane flying under IFR. I called them on the radio.."

"Excuse me. What does IFR mean?"

"Sorry. Instrument Flight Rules. If a plane is flying under instruments, then they have to file a flight plan. Anyway, I called them on the radio and then I started over to try and stop them from taking off. They responded by sending a bullet my way. They've just about got both engines warmed enough to taxi."

"Why do you suppose they're trying to get out of here without a flight plan? Any idea what they're carrying?"

"Don't have a clue, detective. The plan flew in a couple of days ago and sat all alone until today. Then two trucks pulled up along side and loaded lots of crates onto the plane. They ditched the trucks on the far side of the runway and then all of them piled into the plane."

"Any idea how many of them there are?" asked Morrison.

"Let's see. There were two big guys, a black guy, what looked like an oriental woman, and the pilot. So there would be five of them."

"Thanks, Reggie. This whole thing is starting to smell, if you ask me. My guys and I will take it from here. You keep the other controllers in the tower. And you keep your head down, too."

"You don't have to tell me twice."

Morrison quickly scanned the area from the doorway. He again ran at a crouch to the car.

"Ok, guys. I think we've come to the right place."

"What do you mean?" I asked.

"I asked how many there were on the plane. The controller told me there were two big buys, a black guy, an oriental woman, and the pilot. Does that remind you of anyone we know."

"If I didn't know any better, I'd say it's our friends from Classic Investments or Royal Realty or whoever the hell they are. With the exception of the pilot. 'Course I guess they would need one, wouldn't they?" said Bill.

"They would. It looks to me like they played us" said Morrison with a trace of disgust in his voice. "They set up the boat deal, hoping we'd fall for it. And like a dumb ass, I did. If they hadn't fired at the controller, we'd still be on our way to the marina."

"Ok, but let's discuss the details later. Right now, we've got to stop that plane. Any ideas?" I asked.

Just then the DC-3s twin engines began to noticeably pick up speed.

"Well, we'd better come up with something pretty damn quick because they're just about ready to taxi" said Bill.

"I like the idea of shooting out one of their tires" suggested Morrison. "Gerr, will that work?"

"Not with our handguns; those tires are too heavy duty. If we had a rifle, then we'd have chance."

"Pop the trunk" yelled the detective. "I've got an M-16 in there. It's that yellow button inside the glove box."

I flipped open the glove compartment and pushed the button. We heard a subdued popping sound and the trunk lid rose two inches. Morrison raised the lid and opened a long case inside. He pulled out an M-16 rifle and grabbed a loaded up magazine. Ducking back down behind the car, he lined the magazine up with the magazine well and slammed it home. Pulling the charging handle, he chambered a .223 caliber round.

"All right, Gerr. You drive. Bill, you get in the front and navigate. I'll be in the back seat trying to take out at least one tire. Let's go, guys."

Gerry slid across the seat and twisted the key. Bill crouched down and moved up to the front seat. Morrison got in the back seat and rolled down the window.

"Let's go. Oh, shit. They're moving. Come on, floor it!"

I jammed the accelerator to the floor and charged after the plane. I circled around onto its left side and slowly began catching up with it. However, the DC-3 was getting up to taxi speed.

"Come on. Give her some more gas; we've got to match their speed" cried Bill.

I finally caught up to the airplane. Morrison stuck the rifle out the rear window and tried to take aim.

"Better start shooting soon, Dave. The DC-3's a tail dragger; once they get up to the speed that they can lift the tail off the runway, they'll be wheels up in seconds" I said.

"All right, all right. Just keep her steady, will you?"

"Gerr, speed up just a little. Dave needs to lead the shot a little" cried Bill.

I edged the car a little faster. Bang! A shot rang out and a bullet tore into the rear fender of the sedan.

"Hey, they're shooting at us!" Bill yelled.

Bang, bang, bang! Three more shots rang out in quick succession. Only these had been fired by Morrison. More shots rang out from the plane. A couple hit the front fender and one shattered the passenger side mirror, just missing Bill and lodging itself into the left hand kick panel in front of my legs.

"Hey, that was a little too close. Come on, Dave. Take these bastards tires out" Bill yelled.

The airplanes small rear wheel slowly rose off of the runway. She was now up on the main landing gear, very quickly approaching take off speed.

Morrison lined up the sights on the M-16 once again. This time he held the trigger back and the rifle began to spray bullets in five second bursts. The left side tire on the DC-3 literally exploded. Shreds of rubber flew high into the air.

The left side landing gear hit the runway and dug deep into the tarmac. The entire left side of the plane dipped and the wing tip caught the tarmac as well. The plane began to cartwheel down the runway, tearing itself apart.

"Gerr, hit the brakes, NOW! We'll be crushed!"

I slammed on the brakes, locking up all four wheels. The car nose dived and smoke rolled off the tires as they slid across the pavement. Finally the sedan came to a stop.

The plane had made one complete cartwheel and half of another. It stopped with the nose down, its tail pointed straight up in the air. It stood there for a split second and then it fell, crashing hard onto its belly.

"Let's get 'em, fellows!" yelled Morrison as he threw open the car door and took off at a run. Bill and I followed close behind.

We all reached the wreck of the plane about the same time. The port side engine had been torn completely away and thrown clear. The starboard engine, still attached, was smoking heavily. Fuel leaked profusely from the wing tanks.

"Let's get 'em out before this thing blows" I yelled. I grabbed at the door handle and tried to pull it open. "It's stuck!"

"Here, let me try" replied Bill. He grabbed the handle and twisted as hard as he could. "It's no good. It must be jammed inside."

Morrison ran around the wing to the front of the plane. The front windows were totally smashed out. "I'm going in" he yelled back to us.

He carefully picked his way through the window, avoiding the jagged shards of glass. Safely there, he surveyed the inside of the airplane.

"It's too dark in here" he yelled. "Gerr, you have your flashlight with you?"

"Yeah, here. I'll throw it to you."

Morrison stuck his head back out of the windshield. I flipped my pocket flashlight up to the waiting detective. He turned it on and played it around the cockpit. There was only one body there, the pilot strapped into his seat. Morrison laid his first two fingers along side of the man's neck to feel for a pulse. It was faint but there was one present. Leaving the man, he opened the door separating the cockpit from the cargo bay of the aircraft.

He shined the light around. The inside was a total shambles. Brackets had torn loose from the walls. Crates were strewn everywhere. Bodies had been tossed around like rag dolls. He turned the light to the door. A piece of wall bracket had fallen down behind the latch mechanism and kept it from opening.

"I'll have the door open in a jiffy, guys" he yelled. He pulled the twisted piece of metal from the latch and pushed the door open. "There you are, come on in and help me check these guys out."

Through the now open doorway, sunlight streamed in to better illuminate the interior of the plane. I climbed in and made my way over the strewn crates to Mrs. Malcomb. Her right leg was bent in a very awkward manner that meant it was surely broken. Blood seeped from a large gash in her right arm. Otherwise, she doesn't look too bad, I thought.

Bill was checking out the big man called Butch. He'd been tossed around a great deal but was still breathing. Morrison looked over the other big man. He too, was breathing and didn't appear too badly hurt.

"Where's Randolph?" asked Bill. "I don't see him anywhere."

Morrison played the light around the cargo bay again. Suddenly he saw a leg sticking out from under one of the fallen crates. He quickly hopped over several of the boxes and made his way to the trapped butler.

"He's over here" he exclaimed while waving his arm. "Come help me get this crate off of him."

We climbed over the scattered crates to where Morrison stood. We could see Randolph's right leg smashed under one of the crates. The crate lay diagonally across his body. That's gotta be making it damn hard to breathe, I thought to myself.

I reached down and grabbed a corner of the crate. "Come on, you two. Grab this thing and let's move it!"

Bill and Morrison grabbed the other end of the crate and tried to lift it. It didn't budge.

"Damn, this SOB is heavy!" exclaimed Bill. "How much does this thing weigh?"

"Of course it's heavy. Each bar weighs about twenty seven and a half pounds. I figure there's probably twenty to twenty five bars per crate. Let's see, that's about 700 pounds in each crate" I replied.

"Well, obviously we're going to have to manhandle this thing by ourselves. Gerry, you and Bill grab that end and I'll try to handle this one. Ready? On three, ok? One, two, three."

"Augh! With that, each of us lifted the crate as best we could and dragged it off of Randolph's limp body.

The sound of sirens could be heard screaming in the distance.

"Good, here comes the cavalry" I said. That sound means fire trucks with foam. I've been just a bit worried about that leaking fuel. Hope they brought ambulances, too."

Bill stuck his head out of the open door and looked around. "Yeah, they brought ambulances" he replied.

"Good, now get back in here and let's move the unhurt guys out first. Gerry, grab that fellows legs. Bill, you get the arms. Careful now. I'm going to see about the pilot."

Bill and I followed Morrison's directions while the detective climbed back through the cockpit door. Stepping over some fallen debris, he reached down and unlatched the pilot's seat belt. He ran both hands up and down the pilots left arm and then the right. Then he knelt down and did the same to both legs. Satisfied that no limbs were broken, he pulled the man's arms up and over his shoulder. Carrying the unconscious pilot out of the cockpit, he made his way to the DC-3s doorway. He got there just as the first of the fireman arrived.

"Here, give me a hand with this guy" he exclaimed to the fireman.

The fireman reached up and took the pilot from Morrison. Several more firemen appeared in the doorway. Bill and I already had one of the men outside and were returning for the other.

"You two have done enough!" yelled the fireman who appeared to be in charge. "Back off and let my men finish up here."

Both of us did as we were told. By now the fire trucks had covered the leaking fuel with foam to eliminate any fire danger. The first of the ambulances was backed up to the open doorway. The two large men were already loaded. The pilot lay on a gurney, paramedics hooking up IVs and taking vital signs.

"Hey, there's the pilot" said Bill. "I wonder how he's doing?"

"I don't think we're going to find out at this moment" I replied. "They're loading him up right now."

The paramedics had finished prepping the man and loaded him into the second ambulance. The siren wailed as it sped off towards the hospital.

The next ambulance backed into the space where the previous one had just vacated. Randolph was brought out next and also transported to the hospital.

"That just leaves Mrs. Malcomb" I said. "Hey," I yelled to the firemen inside the plane. "She's got a broken leg and possibly a broken arm as well. Let the paramedics in to splint her up before you move her."

"No problem, send 'em in" replied the lead fireman. "Tell them to hurry, though. She doesn't look too good."

"You heard him!" I exclaimed as I waved the paramedics into the plane. They ran past me and climbed in amongst the scattered crates and twisted metal. Quickly they reached the stricken woman and assessed her situation.

"She'll be ok, guys. We've got the bleeding stopped. We're going to have to get a doctor to reset her leg, though. I can't do anything like that here."

"That's fine, just get her fixed up" said Morrison.

With that, the paramedics got Mrs. Malcomb out of the airplane and loaded into the waiting ambulance. Her leg now stabilized, the generals widow was soon on her way to the hospital as well.

Chapter 32

I grabbed the cordless phone and pushed the talk button to quiet the incessant ringing. I glanced at the wall clock. It read nine fifteen.

"Hello"

"Gerr, this is Dave. Can you grab Bill and meet me at the Gettysburg Hospital? The pilot's finally woken up."

"You bet! We'll be there in forty five minutes."

I hung up the phone for a second and then dialed Bill.

"Hey, Morrison just called. Our pilot is awake. Morrison wants us to meet him at the hospital. I figure he's going to question him."

"Cool. Pick me up?"

"On my way. See you in five."

We both entered the hospital and walked to the information desk.

"May I help you, gentlemen?" asked the blond nurse behind the desk.

"You may" I replied. "We're looking for Detective Morrison. He should be here with one of the victims of the plane crash in York the other day."

"Oh, yes. He said to send you right in. They're in Room 214. You can use the elevator right over there." She pointed to a set of doors diagonally across the hall. "When you get to the second floor, turn left and it's at the end of the hall."

"Thank you very much" I said.

We walked to the elevator. Bill pushed the second floor button and we waited. There was a whirring sound from behind the doors and in a few seconds an elevator car arrived.

We followed the nurses' directions and soon were standing at the door to Room 214. I knocked.

"Come on in, guys" came Morrison's voice from within.

We both walked into the room. Morrison sat in a straight back chair beside the hospital bed.

It was elevated slightly. The occupant sat halfway up in the bed. The top of his head was bandaged as were both arms.

"You??" We both exclaimed at the same time.

"You two know this guy?" asked an incredulous Morrison, a confused look on his face.

"Hell, yes, we know him! That's Colonel Michael Edwards, U.S. Air Force. Now it's all coming together. He was in Germany at the same time as the rest of the Classic Investments mob. Obviously he was in it with them" I exclaimed.

"Yeah. And you probably killed the general too, you rotten bastard!" retorted Bill angrily.

"No, I didn't kill Wilford" replied the colonel. "I couldn't; we were friends, remember? That was Butch."

"So when did you hatch this nefarious plan of yours?" I asked.

"Well, apparently you already know most of it" replied Edwards sarcastically. "Some of us knew each other from 'Nam. The rest we met in Germany. We were all having a few beers one

Saturday when we ran into the old German sailor from the war. He was getting pretty hammered and started to tell us about the gold. We didn't believe him at first, but Sun Lee said she was pretty sure she had heard the story before. So we made notes of everything he said and told ourselves someday when we all got back to the states, we would find that gold."

"Who came up with the Classic Investments idea, anyway?" I asked.

"The initial idea was Randolph's. He's actually a big car guy and he explained to us how easy it would be to counterfeit vintage muscle cars. I did the organizing and pretty soon we were up and running. We made a ton of money off that setup. Then, just for kicks, Randolph decided to hook Will into the scam. He talked him into buying a car or two, giving him this pie in the sky bullshit about how these cars were going to be worth a fortune in a few years."

"The real ones are going to go up in value" Bill interjected.

"Of course they are, you moron. But these are fakes, remember? Try to keep up, kid. So, finally we figured we'd played with him enough.

We went for one last big score. The Corvette Grand Sport. That went well for a while. But then some guy he played golf with told him there were only six built and he started to get suspicious. I told Sun Lee to fix the problem. Apparently she had Butch whack him. Hey, never turn your back on her; she's one cold bitch."

"So what happened then?" asked Morrison.

"Well as you already know, I'm sure, we'd planned way ahead. I set up a dummy realty company and made Randolph the president. With our incredible profits from the old cars, we had plenty of cash to buy some heavy equipment and spread around for public relations purposes. All I had to do was buy a few drinks for the mayor of East Berlin and selling him on the con was a piece of cake."

"Ok, guys. Now we're getting to the bottom of this. At least we know who he is now. Now we can finish putting two and two together" replied Morrison. "In fact, how about we step outside for a moment?"

Morrison rose from his chair and motioned for us to follow him. When we were outside,

Morrison pulled out his cell phone and pushed a button.

"Jefferies? Yeah, it's me. Listen, we know who the suspect that was driving the plane is. I want you to send a guard over here to the hospital and put him on the door of Room 214. Nobody except hospital staff gets in. Or out. No one, got that? I'm detaining this guy pursuant to arrest. I've got him handcuffed to the bed rail so he's not going anywhere at the moment. Good, get on it immediately."

"Now, guys, let's get down to the station and sort this out. I think we have enough now to put together a pretty good case of first degree murder for Butch and accessory to murder for the rest of the bunch. Let's go down to the nurse's desk and see what room Butch is in."

We all walked down the corridor to the closest nurse's station.

"Excuse me" said Morrison. "Could you tell me which room Butch is in?"

The nurse looked through her records and tapped on some keys on the computer keyboard. "I'm sorry sir, we don't have anyone by the name of 'Butch' here. We generally don't go by nicknames. You'll need his complete, real name if you want me to be able to find him."

"Oh, yeah. I forgot. Gerry, what the hell was Butch's real name anyway?"

"White, Frederick White. That's his real name."

"Oh, I'm sorry sir, that gentleman was treated and released."

"What? How the hell could you do that?" exclaimed the detective.

"I'm not sure I like your tone of voice, sir" she retorted with a shake of her head. "We didn't have any reason to keep him. You cops never said keep him. Or the other gentleman, for that matter. Our job is to patch them up. That's what we did. He paid the bill and walked out. If you wanted him, you should have arrested him or detained him or whatever you cops do. It's not our fault."

"Ok, ok. You're right. Geesh, don't get your knickers in a twist, lady. I didn't mean to piss you off. Sorry, ok?"

Without waiting for an answer, Morrison turned and strode off briskly. Bill and I followed close behind.

"Whoa, slow down. Where do you suppose he went?"

"I wouldn't have a clue. What a dumb ass I am. I should have had a guard on his door. And Lou's. Now they're both in the wind. My god, how stupid could I be?" Morrison replied in disgust. "A rookie wouldn't have made a dumb ass mistake like that."

"Hey look, you can kick your own ass later. Right now we've got to figure out where they went. We know they don't have the gold and there's no chance they're going to get it. So, they're going to need money to get out of the country" I said.

"That makes sense" replied Morrison as we reached the front doors of the hospital. He reached out, grabbed the door handle, and held it open for us. "That only leaves one place where they could possibly have a large amount of cash on hand; the Malcomb mansion."

"Problem is, they've got a day head start. If they went there straight from the hospital, they've already got the cash. Where on earth are we going to start looking?"

We reached our cars. Morrison pulled open the door of his sedan and plopped down into the drivers' seat.

"I think we should pop on over to the station and start there. I'll call the cops out in Monroeville and see if they'll go around to the house and check it out" he said.

"That sounds like a pretty good idea. We'll follow you."

Chapter 33

The red phone began ringing. Morrison grabbed it on the third ring. I glanced up at the row of clocks on the wall of the command center. The east coast clock read two fifteen in the afternoon.

"Yes, this is Morrison. What? They did?" He listened for a few minutes. "Ok, thanks very much. I really appreciate it, fellows."

"Well, we're too late. They've been there and gone. The Monroeville cops found a hidden room in the library. There was a ham radio and a safe inside. The safe was open and, of course, empty. We have no way of knowing what else besides cash was in there, but of course there's a damn good chance there were extra passports as well."

"Wonderful" I replied. "They could be anywhere. Hell, they could even be out of the country by now."

"I don't know about that" Bill said. "I think they're going to play it cool. They probably figure we'll have the airports watched. Same goes for train stations and bus terminals. They still need to get out of the country, though. I'd bet they're going to travel by private car."

"Not bad. Makes sense. Now all we have to do is figure out where" I replied.

"Well, I'd say there's a better than average chance they'll go with Plan B. Remember how they fooled us with the boat deal? They made us think they were going to escape by boat. Suppose that wasn't just a ruse? Suppose that was actually Plan B. Don't forget, this whole bunch are all ex-military. I'm pretty sure they would have had a secondary plan to fall back on" said Morrison. "Jefferies" he yelled.

The young deputy stuck his head around the corner. "Yes, Detective?"

"Call Harford County, Maryland. Tell them to get out to that marina and look for Butch and Lou."

"10-4, boss. I'm on it."

Morrison grabbed his hat and motioned to us. "Let's go, we might as well head over that way, too."

We hurried through the door and into the parking lot. Morrison broke into a trot, headed to his car.

"Come on, you two ride with me."

We changed our direction and made for Morrison's sedan.

"Shotgun" yelled Bill.

"Really? You're calling 'shotgun'? Are you crazy?" I asked as we ran full speed.

"Sorry, Gerr. I must have flashed back to our youth."

"Would you two just get in the damn car?" yelled Morrison. "We haven't got all day."

I jumped into the front passenger seat while Bill piled into the rear. Morrison already had the motor running. He grabbed the shifter and yanked it down. Morrison skillfully guided it out of the parking lot and into traffic. He headed down Route 30 towards York.

The sun was behind us by the time we reached the intersection at Cross Keys. The light over the intersection was glowing red as traffic began slowing.

"Hey, look up there" I pointed to a car five cars ahead of us. "I think we just lucked out."

There, just ahead, sat an orange Pontiac GTO Judge idling at the light.

"Well, well, well. That sure looks like the Judge we saw back at Wendals Garage, doesn't it, Gerr?" asked Bill.

"I would have to say, as Morrison did earlier, there's a better than average chance that it is" I replied. "Dave, how do you want to 'take them down', as you cop types like to say?"

"Well, I hate the idea of letting them get too far; they could possibly give us the slip. But I don't want to risk a lot of lives in a wild car chase, either. I guess we'll just keep following them and play it by ear."

We followed the GTO through Abbottstown and the tiny hamlet of Thomasville. We went past the York Airport and then approached the expressway split that turned the Lincoln Highway into a three and four lane expressway through York city. The GTO didn't take the expressway, however. It stayed on the old, original Route 30 which turned into Market Street.

"Where do you suppose they're going?" asked Bill. "The main highway went that way." He pointed to our left.

"I wouldn't have a clue. This leads downtown. It's sure not the quickest way to the marina" replied Morrison.

"You don't think they made us, do you? Maybe they're leading us on a wild goose chase" I said.

"No. I don't think there's much chance of that. No, I think they came this way for a reason. I just don't know what it is. Yet."

We followed for several more blocks. Suddenly the Judges' left turn signal began to blink. The bright orange car started to make its turn.

"Well, that's something I hadn't figured on" I said. "They're going to a tin indian convention!"

"A what?" exclaimed Morrison.

"A tin Indian convention. Look!" I pointed to the sign. It read 'Welcome Pontiac Owners Club' and was hanging over the entrance to the York Fairgrounds.

"You mean to tell me we've been following Butch and Lou to a Pontiac Owners Club meet?" Morrison asked incredulously.

"If that is, in fact, Butch and Lou. That *could* be a different car. Do you realize how many goats are going to be at this show?" I replied.

"Goats? Tin Indians? What the hell for language are you speaking?" demanded Morrison.

"Goats are slang for GTOs. Tin Indians are slang for Pontiacs. Where were you in the '60s, Dave?"

"I was in school learning normal English, apparently. Well, we're going in here and check it out."

Morrison turned into the fairgrounds entrance as well. He followed the orange GTO until it pulled onto the show field and parked in a section with about two hundred other Pontiacs. We parked in the spectator's lot and got out.

"Let's go look the car over and check out the owner. I think we should just walk around and look like interested spectators. That way we can ask questions about the cars and not arouse any suspicions. Flashing badges is bound to be counterproductive around here" I said.

"Yeah, I think that's a good idea" Morrison replied.

We walked across the street to the show field. Bill and I gravitated directly to a 1964 GTO convertible that just happened to be sitting next to our suspect car. Morrison got caught up looking over a gorgeous 1967 Grand Prix convertible. Bill and I moved over to the GTO we'd been following.

"Say, buddy, that's a fine looking Judge. Have it long?" I asked the middle age man who appeared to be showing the car.

"You bet. I bought this right out of high school. Did a full frame up restoration two years ago. I paid $4,300 for it brand new and I wouldn't sell it for any amount now. Look, here's my original bill of sale."

"Wow! That's incredible. Hey, listen we have a lot more cars to look at, so if you don't mind, we'll talk to you later."

Bill and I walked off and looked at a few other cars while we waited for Morrison to catch up.

"Hey, guys. Did you know that '67 was the only year for the Grand Prix convertible? I had no clue. Man, I learned a lot from that guy" said Morrison as we regrouped.

"Yes, Dave. We knew that. You weren't supposed to take an entire semester of automotive history. You were just supposed to make small talk while we got info from the guy with the GTO Judge."

"How do you guys know so much about cars? Anyway, what did you learn from that guy?"

"He's not our man. He's owned that car for the past forty some years. We better get back to the original plan. Back to the car, guys."

Chapter 34

"Look, Dave, it's not your fault. Ok, we lost a lot of time. But we all thought that was the car we were looking for. It sure looked like it. Do you have any idea how many Judges were painted Carousel Red in 1969? A hell of a lot. It was an honest mistake."

"I thought it was orange?"

"Well, it's officially named Carousel Red, paint code 72. That's not what's important right now. Right now we have to find the bad guys."

"How *do* you guys know so much about cars?"

"We just do; we've been gear heads since we were kids, ok? Now, how about burning some rubber?"

Morrison responded by burying the accelerator. The needle on the speedometer rose accordingly. We were back on the Lincoln Highway now and making up for lost time dramatically.

"Ok, we're almost to the river. Now pay attention. I know where I'm going, but it's been a while since I've been down here. The marina is at a campgrounds, way down river, just over the border in Maryland. There are a lot of twists and turns between here and there, so be careful but still go as fast as you dare" said Bill.

"Right, you're the official navigator" replied Morrison.

We flew down the back roads as fast as Morrison could make the sedan go and still stay on the asphalt.

"Turn right here. Ok, we're only a few miles from the marina.

We flew down the road. Bill indicated one more turn. Another couple of miles and a boat yard came into view.

"There it is, guys. Dave, pull in the first driveway there. The office is down at the end." Bill pointed to a gravel drive between two rows of boats.

We turned where Bill had indicated and drove to the end. There, on the left, was a rundown building with a hand lettered sign that read 'Office' over the door. Morrison pulled up in front and we all quickly ran inside.

The detective looked around for a bell to ring for service. Seeing none, he pounded on the counter with his right palm. "Is anybody here?"

"Hold yer damned horses!" came a voice from the other room. A grizzled old man with three day old beard stubble appeared from around a corner. "Can't a fellow take a break once in a while?"

"Look, friend. You can go back to your nap as soon as I get a little information. We're looking for a yacht that may have either been moored here or may have come this way recently. Ring any bells?"

"What's it to ya, fellow?"

"I'm a cop, that's what" he said indignantly as he pulled out his badge. "Now, have you seen a yacht around here lately?"

"Yeah, I seen one. 'Bout a thirty five footer. But it ain't here now. It was for about a week. But two guys showed up about half an hour ago and shoved off."

"You mean they only have a half hour head start? You got a fast boat we can use?"

"I got a pretty good one out there. It's got a pair of two hundred horse Yamaha's on it. It ain't no cigarette boat, but it's pretty damn fast. Here's the key. It's the red and white one three slips down." He laid a key chain with an orange float on the counter. "Always glad to help law enforcement."

"Thanks, bud. We'll take care of her for you. Let's go, guys."

We exited the door and broke into a trot towards the boat.

"That was pretty civic minded of the old guy" said Bill. "He didn't even balk a little bit when you asked to borrow his boat."

"He knew better" replied Morrison. "That stuff he was drinking didn't come out of a store bought container, if you catch my drift. That was some homemade corn liquor, so he knew better than to object."

We found the boat and jumped in. Morrison fired up the twin outboards while I cast off the mooring lines and then jumped aboard. No sooner than I got in my seat, Morrison jammed both throttles forward and the boat leapt away from the dock. He steered out into the middle of the current and pointed the nose downstream. The boat picked up speed dramatically. Soon we were being battered around violently by the boat bouncing across on the waves. The spray hit us all square in the face.

"How far ahead do you think they are?" I asked.

"Well, they have no way of knowing that we're following them. So I figure they're just putting along in that big old yacht. If I keep this thing wide open, I figure we'll catch them before they make the Bay."

We began to pass the occasional boat. Most were small fishing craft, although there were a few pleasure boats cruising around as well. The closer we got to the Chesapeake Bay, the more boats we started to see.

"Keep an eye out, guys. We could be seeing them any moment now."

As if Morrison were clairvoyant, I suddenly saw a yacht about a quarter of a mile almost directly ahead of us.

"There you go, Dave" I pointed. "That looks like her."

I pitched unexpectedly forward as Morrison closed both throttles abruptly. The bow of the boat took a sudden dive and then leveled itself out. Our boat rolled gently with the waves as Morrison reached into his pocket and brought out his cell phone.

"Hello, operator? Give me the Coast Guard. This is Detective Sergeant Morrison, Adams County, Pennsylvania. Yes, thanks." He waited for a few seconds while the operator connected him with the closet Coast Guard station.

"Hello, detective? This is Lieutenant Commander Wilson, U.S Coast Guard Station, Curtis Bay. What can I do for you?"

"Commander, My deputies and I are following a murder suspect down the Susquehanna River by boat. He is on a yacht with another man who is also wanted. We are just about to enter the Bay. Can you intercept them for us?"

"Not a problem, detective. Can you describe the craft we'll be looking for?"

"Yes sir. It's a white inboard cruiser of about 35 feet. We'll be following it at a discreet distance in a red and white 20 footer with twin outboards."

"Good enough, detective. I'll pass this info along to my patrol boat. Don't worry; they'll find you."

We kept following the yacht. It entered the Chesapeake Bay and kept sailing south. We shadowed them for another hour with no sign of the Coast Guard.

"Well, where do you suppose the Coasties are? If they don't show up soon, we're going to have to find a place to stop for fuel. Those guys can keep on going; that thing holds a hell of a lot of fuel" said Morrison.

"I'm sure they'll be here" I replied. "They may have been delayed."

Finally, about ten minutes later, a 25 foot Coast Guard patrol boat came into view from the south. As they got close to the yacht, their red and blue lights began to flash and the siren began to wail. A few seconds later, we heard a voice directed at the yacht through a megaphone.

"This is the United States Coast Guard. Southbound yacht, heave to and prepare to be boarded! I repeat, heave to and prepare to be boarded!"

The yacht slowed appreciably. The patrol boat pulled up along the starboard side, it's red, inflatable sides gently cushioning the yacht, so as not to scratch it. Morrison brought our boat along the port side. He and I climbed onto the yacht while Bill held our boat steady alongside. We could hear the Coast Guardsmen talking to one of the two men aboard the yacht.

"That's Lou doing the talking. Where's Butch?" I whispered to Morrison.

"I don't know" he whispered back. "I don't like this. Let's look around but be quiet and be careful."

I nodded and crept aft. I eased myself along side of the cabin and occasionally I peered inside. All of a sudden, I saw Butch crouched down behind a bulkhead, holding what appeared to be a Heckler and Koch MP-5 submachine gun. He was

273

intently watching Lou speaking with the Coast Guardsmen. He's going to gun them down, I said to myself. I looked back for Morrison, but he was sneaking off in the opposite direction, towards the bow of the craft.

I could tell Butch was getting anxious by the way he was fidgeting with his trigger finger. I knew it was now or never; he was about ready to start spraying 9 millimeter rounds all over the Coast Guardsmen. I had no choice.

I yelled at the top of my lungs "Butch, drop the gun!" He turned, pointing the MP-5 directly at me. I already had my Sig in my hand. Once more, I yelled "Drop it!" Butch's finger clinched the trigger and the submachine gun spat 9 millimeter bullets, stitching a neat row of bullet holes in the paneling directly over my head. I raised my Sig and, squeezing the trigger twice, put two hollow point rounds into his center mass. He dropped the gun, grabbed his chest, and doubled over.

As soon as I yelled, Lou turned and saw Morrison. A pistol appeared, seemingly out of nowhere, in Lou's hand. Morrison saw it and immediately put several rounds from his 40 caliber Glock into Lou's midsection. Lou dropped to his knees, stayed there for a second, and then fell face forward onto the deck with a thud. The young Coast Guard Lieutenant, who had just been conversing with Lou, stared at both of us with a shocked look covering his face.

"It's ok Lieutenant. We're the good guys. I'm Detective Sergeant Morrison and this is my deputy, Gerry Campbell. If you'll excuse us, right now we'd better clear the rest of the vessel before go any farther."

Morrison and I went below and swept the rest of the boat for any other individuals who may have been on board. The boat was clear; we found no one else hiding anywhere.

A Coast Guard corpsman was just finishing up checking Lou's body when we arrived back topside. "They're both dead, sir" he said to his lieutenant. "Appears instantaneous."

"Thanks, doc." He turned to Morrison. "I'd say thank you's are in order all around, detective. If you and your deputy hadn't acted as you did, we'd all be dead. With the kind of firepower these two were packing, we wouldn't of had a snowballs chance in hell. That bastard there would have cut us to pieces with that automatic."

"Just doing our job, Lieutenant. We couldn't have done it without your help."

Chapter 35

"Worldwide Locator, Chief Lucas, May I help you?"

"Chief, Master Sergeant Campbell. We got them! We got the whole gang! And, just as we promised, you're the first to know. Mrs. Malcomb and Randolph are in jail. Lou and Butch are dead. Butch was the one who actually killed General Malcomb. And the ringleader was no other than Colonel Michael Edwards."

"Edwards, the ringleader? Wow, sarge. I would have never figured that one. Lou, Butch, and Randolph – well, they don't surprise me at all. Sun Lee, I can't say I'm terribly surprised about her, either. I never quite trusted her; although I really didn't have any solid reason that I could put my finger on. Well, I must say, you two did one hell of a job. I really appreciate what you've done. Not just for me, but for all of us in the Air Force. All of us who served under General Malcomb and all of us who looked up to and respected the man. Thank you again, sarge."

"Chief, we couldn't have done it without you. You were as important to this investigation as any one of us. Never forget that."

"Thanks, sarge. That's something I never will forget."

Chapter 36

"You know something, Gerr, I think we've earned ourselves a drink. How about we stop by the club on the way home?"

"That's not a bad idea, Bill. I like it. Ok, since we're in separate cars, I'll just meet you there."

"Sounds good to me. See you there."

We left the station and met twenty minutes later at our favorite club. I got there first; well, I was driving the Corvette. I went in and found us a table. Bill arrived a minute or two later.

"What'll you have?" asked the nattily attired waitress who suddenly appeared at our table.

"I'll have a Sam Adams" I said. "Bill?"

"I'd better stick with Lite. Gotta watch my figure, you know."

"Thanks, I'll be right back, guys." With that, she left for the bar to get our drinks.

While we waited for our beer, I looked around the club. As usual, the lights were rather low. I recognized most of the regulars at the bar. There were several couples I didn't know sitting together at a table in the corner. All of a sudden, my eye caught a familiar sight.

"Oh my god! Bill, look over there. At the end of the bar. No, don't gawk. It's that blonde from my dreams. Oh, hell. She's seen us. I think she's going to come over here."

And sure enough, she was. The voluptuous blond was making her way slowly over to our table. Her ample bosom strained against the low cut neckline of the red satin dress she wore, the same one she always wears in my dreams. Hard, perky nipples pushed outward on each breast. Her tight, round buttock gently swayed from side to side as she seemed to simply glide between the chairs. I politely rose from my chair as she approached.

"Would you like a drink?" I asked.

"I'd just love an apple martini" she replied coyly.

I desperately looked around the bar for a waitress. Suddenly I saw one by the name of April come around the corner from one of the private dining rooms. I motioned for her to come to our table.

"Hi, Gerry. May I help you?"

"Sure. This young lady would like an apple martini."

"Then she shall have one. Be right back, Gerry."

"Oh, April? Would you do me a favor?" asked Bill.

"Sure. What can I do?"

"Have the bartender cancel my Lite. I don't think Gerry needs a third at this little party. Gerr, she didn't fade away this time; it could be the start of something beautiful. Good luck."

And with that, Bill rose from his chair and, with a coy little wink, walked away.